this i

END,
baby

epilogue novella

Mandy,
Happy endings aren't
for villains ...
♡ K Webster

K WEBSTER

This is the End, Baby
Copyright © 2017 K. Webster

ISBN-13: 978-1546499480
ISBN-10: 1546499482

Cover Design: All By Design
Photo: Adobe Stock
Editor: Prema Editing
Formatting: Champagne Formats

M,

Thanks for putting up with me...

Even when I'm as psycho as Hannah Bananas.

YOURS until the END, baby.

K

War and Peace Series Reading Order

"When love is not madness, it is not love."
—Pedro Calderón de la Barca

Warning:

This is the End, Baby is a dark romance. Extreme sexual themes and violence, which could trigger emotional distress, are found in this story. If you are sensitive to dark themes, then this story is not for you. *This is the End, Baby* is the seventh and final book in the series. Please read the first six books before reading this one to fully understand the story.

Dear Reader,

Thank you for going on this epic and twisted journey with me! Your support has been amazing! I ask that you PLEASE don't spoil the plot or ending of this book in your reviews. I want everyone to be just as surprised as you. The twists and turns are designed for your enjoyment. They aren't as fun when you know what they are going in. Thank you so much for helping me with this!

Sincerely,
K Webster

PROLOGUE

Hannah

HIS DARK HAIR IS SOFT. SO SOFT. I COULD STARE at him for hours while he sleeps. Sometimes I do. He's beautiful and mine. Every night, when I look at him, I am reminded that I am happy. *He* makes me happy.

Other times, he maddens me.

I can't pinpoint it exactly. It isn't any one thing. Just that his presence rubs me the wrong way. Every day, it worsens. I don't like that feeling at all.

I stroke his hair again and murmur, "I love you."

It's times like these I have to remind myself that I *do* love him. That he *is* mine. I have to remind myself that I am in charge of my thoughts…the darkness is *not* in charge of me.

I close my eyes and start to hum a song I remember Mom humming when I was a child. It would always calm me when I was in the middle of a tantrum. For as long as I can remember, my mother and I have always butted heads. It's only recently that we've talked a little more. We mostly tolerate each other. You'd think Gabe would be a deal breaker for her, but she puts up with him. Despite everything that went on between them in the past, she welcomes him into her home.

It makes me wonder if she still has feelings for him.

I often wonder if Dad were to suddenly die, would she go after my husband?

Would she remember what a good lover he was and want that back?

Anger bubbles up inside my chest. Mom is beautiful and looks younger than her actual age. She runs most days and eats well. If she wanted to seduce him, she probably could.

I try to imagine her as a teen having sex with my husband. Thoughts of my mother beneath him moaning his name have me fisting my hand and gritting my teeth. I can almost hear her moans.

Gabe…

Gabe…

More…

"Sweet girl?"

I snap my eyes open and cast an irritated glare at him. That perfect mouth has been on my mother's pussy. He's been inside her.

"Hannah," he utters as he strides into Land's nursery. "Let me put him back in his crib and then we can go back to bed."

I stop gliding in the rocker but don't release my baby to him. His eyes narrow but he doesn't challenge me. Instead, my sleepy husband drops to his knees and hugs us both. Some of the tension releases from my chest. While Land sleeps in one of my arms, I can't help but reach over with my free hand and stroke Gabe's hair.

"How are you feeling?" he asks, his voice muffled against my breast.

"Just thinking about things."

He tilts his head up. "What things?"

I frown and dart my eyes over to the window. "Things that make me angry."

His fingers grip my jaw and he turns my head to look down at him. "What things, baby?"

"You and Mom," I seethe, the accusation heavy in my voice.

"She and I were over before you were even

conceived." His brows furl together and an annoyed sigh escapes him. "We've been through this a thousand times."

My tone is bitter. "I'm your second choice."

"Hannah," he warns. "How many times—"

"Daddy?"

He and I both jerk our heads around to see our sleepy toddler standing in the doorway, rubbing her eyes. My heart warms to see her in her cute pink polka-dot zip-up pajamas. Her blond curls are fuzzy from sleep. She's been wandering a lot more in the middle of the night and early mornings since we recently switched her from her crib to a toddler bed.

"Come here, Toto," I coo and motion for her.

Gabe twists to sit on his butt with his back against my shins. Toto walks over and climbs into his lap. He holds her against his chest and strokes her soft hair. A smile plays at my lips. She reaches a small hand up, and I grab it. Land stirs but doesn't wake.

"*We* are a family, Hannah," Gabe murmurs, but his tone is fierce. "You and I and these babies."

My eyes sting but tears don't form. Sometimes I hate that I'm broken. The emotions that normal people have aren't in my hollow chest anymore. They've dried up and crumbled away. Anger is my most prevalent emotion. It feels like it takes over more often than not.

"I hate being sick," I hiss as though the words themselves are tainted.

A growl rumbles from my husband. "You're not sick…you're just in desperate need of a vacation."

Toto peers over her father's shoulder at me with her big brown eyes and smiles. It reminds me of Gabe. The love in that smile nearly knocks the breath out of me.

"Are you going to take me on vacation so you can off me and dump me somewhere in the Pacific Ocean?" I question, my voice only half teasing in nature. "Then find a new wife? Someone normal?"

Toto smiles shyly at me again. Those smiles are distracting. A trick she most definitely learned from her daddy.

"I'm not even entertaining those questions with an answer. I love you more than anything in this world," he grumbles. "You know this."

"I love you, Mommy," Toto agrees.

My heart expands, and I grin at her. "I love you too, baby."

She starts whining to climb into my lap, so Gabe sets her on her feet so he can relieve me of the baby. As soon as Land is in his daddy's arms, Toto crawls into my lap. Her small hands touch my face as she beams at me. I run my fingers through her messy hair and study her features.

Her light blonde hair is soft. So soft. I could stare at her for hours while she watches me with her cute grins and adoring eyes. Sometimes I do. She's beautiful and mine. Every day, when I look at her, I am reminded that I am happy. *She* makes me happy.

Other times, she maddens me.

I can't pinpoint it exactly. It isn't any one thing. Just that her presence rubs me the wrong way. Every day, it worsens. I don't like that feeling at all.

I stroke her hair again and murmur, "I love you."

After Land is back in his crib, Gabe stares out the window for a long time with his strong arms crossed over his chest and his back to me. After some time, Toto falls asleep. I stand and carry her back to her bedroom. Once I've kissed her and shut the door behind me, I start down the hallway.

I sense his heat before he even touches me. A moment later, a hand covers my mouth from behind, and I'm captured in his powerful arms.

His mouth finds my ear, and I shiver when he nips at my lobe with his teeth. "You have to stay out of that head of yours and with me, sweet girl. It's the only way for us to be happy."

I whimper when his free hand slides to my

breast through my silky gown. He trails kisses down the side of my neck before releasing me to twist me around. His dark eyes are narrowed as his palm grips my throat. My head thumps the wall when he pushes me against it. I love when he possesses me. He keeps me focused on what matters. Us.

"God, sweet girl," he mutters as he nips at my bottom lip and chin and jaw. "You have to get your shit together. You *have* to."

"I'm trying," I promise as I grip his hair to guide him down to my aching breasts. He bites my nipple through the fabric and regards me with a wicked glare that makes my panties wet. I tug his hair to the left so he'll bite my other nipple too.

His chocolate brown hair is soft. So soft. I could stare at him for hours while he devours me, his touches demanding and consuming. Sometimes I do. He's beautiful and mine. Every day, when I look at him, I am reminded that I am happy. *He* makes me happy.

Other times, he maddens me.

I can't pinpoint it exactly. It isn't any one thing. Just that his presence rubs me the wrong way. Every day, it worsens. I don't like that feeling at all.

I stroke his hair again and murmur, "I love you."

1 | Gabe

S MUCH AS I LOVE THE BEACH, I KNOW WE CAN'T live here forever. This home doesn't meet our needs anymore. We're too close to people. Hannah doesn't do well around people.

"We've tried everything on the market," War complains on the other end of the line.

I run my fingers through my hair and huff in frustration. "So we try everything *not* on the market. Come on, man, you have access to this shit. Find something. Anything. It's absolutely necessary we find a solution."

He's quiet for a moment, and I listen for Land. Thankfully he's still napping, so I can keep my focus on Hannah and Toto playing in the sand not two hundred feet from where I stand inside the house.

"Is it getting worse?"

Worse? Hannah is always worse than the day before. But this is different. This is darker and more unpredictable.

"I can't read her anymore," I hiss. "She's a fucking live wire, and I am scared as hell it'll be one of the kids that gets hurt."

I hear him tapping away on his keyboard but he remains silent. Then he sighs. "Have you thought about putting her back in an institution?" Even though he says the words, which sound like scripted shit straight from Baylee's mouth, I know that isn't what he wants.

"Fuck the institutions," I snap. "I told you how she was when I took her from the one Baylee sent her to. My sweet girl was so fucked in the head. They were supposed to make her better, not pump her full of bullshit that makes her talk to goddamned walls. She will not ever go to an institution in my lifetime."

His tapping stops. "I don't know that I like where this conversation is going."

"Fuck you, War. You know that if you don't get your shit together and find something that works, my hands will be tied. I'll be forced to do something neither of us wants. She's the fucking mother of my children. You think I want to hurt her?"

"Touch her and I'll—"

"You'll what, man? Turn me in?" I rub the tension from the back of my neck. "This isn't just about her. It's about my fucking kids."

"Bay and I can keep them. Send them to us, and we'll raise them. Take her somewhere safe. Just don't hurt her," he pleads.

I swallow and dart my gaze out to see Toto running circles around her mother, squealing with laughter as Hannah tries to tickle her. "I can't do that. I can't not see my kids. I already made that fucking mistake once with Brie. I won't do it again."

Land fusses in the other room but doesn't cry yet.

"I'll intensify my searches. I can go on the deep web and hunt for something on the black market. I'll keep digging." His chair creaks and he grumbles. "But this shit isn't tested, Gabe. I have no idea what the side effects will be. We're playing with fire, and it involves my daughter—"

"She's my fucking wife! You think I don't know this already?" I snarl. My outburst makes Land start to cry. I stalk into his bedroom. "Time is running out. You should have seen her last night. It's getting fucking creepy. One of these days, I feel like she's going to snap."

Land squirms in his crib but his cries lessen when he sees me.

"Hey there, baby boy," I coo as I scoop him into my arms and pull him against my chest. I redirect my attention to War on the phone as I walk back over to the window to watch my girls who are outside. "Just keep looking."

He sighs. "I will. Also, I was going to tell you when I had more information but I think I found what you were looking for. It's a hunch, based on some cryptic texts, but I believe it's what you're searching for."

My chest tightens. "You have a location?"

"I do. Like I said, it hasn't been one hundred percent verified, but all signs point to it. Are you really going to do it?" he questions.

I kiss Land's soft forehead while he gnaws on his fist. He's hungry, and I'll need to have Hannah come back in to feed him soon. "Of course I am."

"What about Hannah?"

"I'm going to take her with me this time. She needs to get away," I tell him. "I think it will be good for her for it to be just her and I for a few days. Plus, it's a helluva lot easier keeping her in line when it's just the two of us."

"Bring my grandbabies over, and we'll keep them. It needs to be done, and she certainly needs a break," he agrees. "Do I need to procure new fake IDs or are the last ones still okay?"

Translation: *Did my innocent little girl murder anyone while using her last ID?*

"They're fine. Book us a flight and find us a hotel. We'll leave as soon as we can. I'm not sitting on this," I order. Land grins up at me, slobber running down his chin. I grin back at him. Cute as fuck little boy.

"On it," War assures me.

I smirk and give him some shit because, why the hell not? "Most fathers would not approve of this."

He grunts. "Spare me the lesson on morality, Gabe. You and I both know the rules are different with Hannah. Not to mention, if it weren't you going to deal with this, my son would be on the first plane out of here."

A smile tugs at my lips. That Ren kid is all right in my book. "Maybe we could invite him along—"

"Don't start," he snaps. "I'll text you with the details."

He hangs up and I chuckle. That is, until I don't see my girls. A quick scan of the beach tells me they aren't there anymore. Panic rises in my chest, and I dart for the sliding glass door. Just as I pull it open, Toto and Hannah bounce over from the side of the house, screaming "Gotcha!"

5

Land lets out a peal of laughter, and Toto runs to hug me around my knees. Hannah's blue eyes are glittering with light and love. God, I wish I could keep her like this. These moments are rare. Fucking beautiful, but rare.

"You scared me," I tell them both as I tug at one of Toto's pigtails.

Hannah laughs. "That was the point." She holds her hands out for Land. As soon as he sees her, his legs start kicking. Kid loves his momma.

I usher them inside, and while Hannah feeds Land, I let Toto help me pull out everything we'll need to make lunch.

I love my family.

I love moments like these.

I love my broken wife.

Which is exactly why I need take care of this shit.

"Where are we going?" Hannah questions for the millionth time since I told her about our romantic getaway. "I mean, I know *where* we're going but *what* are we going to do there?"

I palm her thigh just below the hem of her dress

and grin at her. "It's a surprise, sweet girl. We haven't done anything like this in awhile, just the two of us. I want you all to myself."

My answer pleases her because she clasps her hand over mine and teases me by pulling my hand further up her thigh. The young guy who's been eyeballing her thighs the entire flight discreetly watches our little display. I'd offered her the seat by the window, but she wanted the middle. My wife likes the attention.

The cabin lights have been dimmed, and many people are sleeping. But not this guy in our row. It's as if he's been waiting for me to fall asleep so he can chat my wife up. I'll give him something to talk about.

My eyes meet Hannah's as I slip my palm under her dress. She spreads her knees to grant me access, bumping the other guy's knee in the process. He lets out a choked sound and shifts uncomfortably in his chair.

I smirk as I run my finger along the outside of her panties where her clit is. A gasp of pleasure escapes her. When I glance over at the guy, who's closer to her age than I am, he's staring shamelessly at the way my hand moves under her dress.

My Hannah is naughty because she likes putting

on a little show.

I lean forward and bite her tit through her dress, my eyes finding the horny guy's beside her. He gives me a deer-in-the-headlights stare as I nip at my woman. The glare I give him back says, *You can watch as long as you don't fucking touch.*

He hisses out a breath of air and slouches in his seat, his palm covering his crotch. Fucking pervert.

"Your panties are wet, sweet girl," I murmur, my breath hot against her dress.

She smiles at me. "They are."

"Does it turn you on that some guy is watching your husband touch you?" I question, my eyebrow lifting.

Her blue eyes flicker with darkness, and she nods. The guy beside her groans.

"Do you want my finger inside your slippery cunt?"

I lift up and scan the cabin for anyone noticing our little party, but nobody is. Nobody but Horny Fuck next to her. I grab hold of her panties and start inching them down. She lifts her ass to help, and together we slide them down her thighs.

When I pull them off her ankles, I hold them out to Horny Fuck. "Can you hold these a second?"

He stares at me with flames of desire flickering

in his eyes and he takes the panties. Who wouldn't? This girl is a fucking knockout. Tall. Blonde. Legs for days. And a rack that most men would only dream of getting to come all over. Once he has her panties in his fist with his other hand resting on his crotch, I slide my palm back under her dress.

"Spread them further," I whisper and lean in to bite her ear lobe.

She does but the space doesn't allow for much room. Her leg lifts and she hooks it over Horny Fuck's thigh. "I hope you don't mind," she purrs at him.

He grips her panties so tight his knuckles turn white. I almost start laughing. He's probably imagining all the ways he'd fuck her. I smirk, knowing she'd fuck *him* up before he even got the chance. She hooks her other leg over my knee and now she's spread wide open for me.

"That's better," I murmur, my tone low and deady, as I slide my finger along her wetness. When I push a finger inside her, she moans softly. I can tell the guy beside me would like to help. I'll rip his entire arm off if he touches her, though.

"You're such a naughty girl," I chide as I slowly fuck her with one finger. "I forgot how naughty you can be."

She whimpers and squirms in the seat. "I need more," she pleads under her breath.

I smirk at Horny Fuck, who is staring at us with his mouth hanging wide open. "How many fingers?"

"All of them," she breathes.

"Jesus Christ," Horny Fuck hisses.

I wink at her as I ease two more fingers into her. My cock is much bigger than three of my fingers. But this girl, with the right amount of lube, has been able to take my entire fist before. She's fucking magical.

"Your body is making so much noise," I observe. Each time I push inside her, her juices make a loud sound. "Maybe we should do something to cover up that sound." When I rub my thumb over her clit, she moans loudly. An old sleeping woman across the aisle stirs but doesn't wake. When I glance back at Horny Fuck, he's discretely rubbing the palm of his hand against his cock, which is hard and noticeable through his sweatpants.

I focus on fingerfucking my wife. She's attempting to be quiet but is having trouble. With my fingers buried in her pussy, she is on the verge of a scream.

"When we get to the hotel," I whisper against her throat, "I'm going to put my dick in your ass. You want that sweet girl?"

"Mmm-hhhmmmm," she moans.

Horny Fuck curses again.

Her legs are beginning to quiver and she has no control over her body. When she runs her heel farther up his thigh, I know it isn't a loss of control. My sweet girl is dirty and likes to make people suffer. The moment her foot touches his cock, I know he's really fucking suffering.

"You're not innocent," I snarl as I nip at her ear. "You're going to fucking pay for that little move."

Her fingers find my hair and she kisses me hard. I know it's to distract me because five bucks says she's trying to get Horny Fuck off with her foot. My girl is dangerous like that. Always playing with fire. She doesn't want that dork. She wants me to punish her for touching him.

"You can't distract me," I hiss as I pull away from our kiss. Sure enough, her foot is rubbing against him, and he's groaning in pleasure. I yank my fingers from her body, causing her to whimper from the loss before I snag the panties from Horny Fuck's fist. "These are mine." Her juices get smeared across the back of his hand in the *exchange*. He gapes at me in horror but then his eyes roll back in his head when she rubs against him again.

I snap my gaze to hers, and she challenges me with her dark stare. I glare at her as I stuff her panties into her mouth. "I need to stifle your scream," I hiss.

My hand goes back under her dress. I get two of my fingers good and wet in her pussy before sliding them to the puckered hole of her ass. She cries out when I push them fully into her. My thumb slips inside her wet cunt and I fuck both holes ruthlessly.

The noises coming from our row are straight up from a porno, and this almost makes me laugh. My own cock is desperate to be inside her, but that'll have to wait until we arrive at the hotel. Horny Fuck just sits back and enjoys a foot rub against his cock.

An old guy in front of us turns to give us a dirty look, but when he sees what we're doing—and most likely gets a firsthand view of what's going on under her dress—he gasps before turning around. Hannah whimpers again and her body begins to tremble. I suck on her earlobe until she's convulsing hard. Her pussy and ass both clench simultaneously around my fingers as she finds her release. Horny Fuck groans too.

They fucking came together.

This makes me snort.

I pull my hand out from under her dress and then yank her knee back to where it belongs—in front of her and away from him. Then, I pull the panties from her mouth and put them in my pocket. Horny Fuck is tense as hell as he stares down at the wet spot soaking through his sweatpants.

"You made a mess there," Hannah says with a loud giggle.

He turns to look at her, his throat turning bright red. If we weren't on an airplane, I'd make his throat *red* all right but with his own blood—brilliant crimson and gushing. Horny Fuck is lucky I'm not free to do what I please. Because it would please me to slaughter him for his part in our little sex show.

"Oh," she says when she notices her wetness smeared on his hand. "That's mine. Sorry about that." She grabs his wrist and brings it to her mouth. Her eyes dart to mine as she licks off the remnants of her arousal from Horny Fuck's hand. When she releases him, he bolts from his chair and all but runs to the bathroom closest to us.

"You're so getting punished for that."

She curls her body to face mine and runs her palm over my cock through my jeans. "Good. I deserve it."

I'm not about to come in my pants like Horny Fuck. So I unzip my jeans and pull my cock out.

"Suck it, bad girl. Hurry."

She leans forward and licks my tip. I grab a handful of her hair as she starts bobbing up and down my

13

length. Her teeth are sharp as she lets them graze along my sensitive flesh. Always reminding me what a fucking monster she can be.

Well, I'm a monster too.

I grip her hair and twist it until I know it hurts. Then, I push her farther down my cock until I feel the head of my dick sliding into her throat. Her throat tenses as she gags but then she relaxes, so I can use her. I make her facefuck me for several long moments until I come with a grunt. My cum rushes down her throat. She doesn't gag but stays relaxed so she can swallow it all down like a good girl.

The old fucker in front of us turns on the light, alerting the stewardess that he needs something. I know the prick just wants to tattle on us. My dick still throbs with its release when I make eye contact with the stewardess who is now making her way toward us.

I release Hannah and she quickly puts my wet cock away. She's just sitting up and righting her dress when the woman asks the old fucker what he needs.

"I need a stiff drink, ma'am," he drawls out.

I smirk and wave at the lady. "Bring one for this row too."

She hustles away, and Horny Fuck shows back up. I can tell he tried to clean up his cum, but it didn't work. He avoids making eye contact with us as he sits back down.

This vacation is already off to one helluva start.

This is exactly what we needed.

II | Hannah

I'M NOT SURE WHY HE BROUGHT US TO THIS seemingly run down city, but at least the hotel is nice, and we have a view of the beach. The pool is killer. While Gabe sleeps, I stare out the window and watch a barge move slowly across the water.

It's peaceful here.

I like it.

My chest aches and I miss my kids. I've been slowly weaning Land off the breast because I haven't been producing as much milk as my hungry boy needs. This trip was the little push he and I both needed to quit for good. But now my breasts are sore. It just reminds me how much I miss having him nurse from me, even if he could only do it once or twice a day.

A buzz comes from Gabe's phone plugged in on the table. Curiosity gets the better of me, and I walk over to see who's texting him.

Brie.

Irritation claws its way up inside of me, but I swallow it down. I vowed I would do my best when it came to Brie. That I'd be nice to her. She has my brother, and they seem happy with the babies. It makes me angry, though, that she now hogs my brother *and* my husband. Stingy bitch.

I read her text to my husband.

Brie Baby: The photographer can do that date. Ren and I have been tasting cakes this week. One more month, Daddy. :)

A huff of breath escapes me, and I roll my eyes. Another little annoyance in my life. Brie and her wedding to my brother. I'm surprised he's so eager to take on some other man's kids. But sweet, stupid Ren dove in without hesitation to play daddy to her twins. Ren was always soft when it came to girls. Always wanted to be the hero.

It was Calder who surprised me. My younger brother fell hard for that chick with no tongue. They actually come over to the house, from time to time, to see Toto and Land. It's Ren and Brie who refuse to see us.

Well, me, actually.

Neither of them want to see me.

I'm not even allowed at their wedding.

Fury surges through me, and I decide I need to let off some steam. I throw on a tank top and some mid-shin-length black workout pants. Once I've laced up my tennis shoes and pulled my long blonde hair into a ponytail, I grab my key from the desk in the room and head out. Despite this hotel being nice enough, it's still old school with real keys. I'd balked at that, but my old man husband didn't even notice until I pointed it out. They were all like this back in the day, he'd said. *The olden days...*

I smirk as I walk down the long hallways on a search for the fitness room we'd passed. When I reach the door, I'm irritated to find it's locked. With a huff, I travel downstairs and through the lobby to go outside.

Today, it's warm out. It'll be dark soon, so I don't want to stay out too late considering I don't know this country very well. We've barely been here a day, and my poor husband is wiped out. After a day of fucking and eating room service, he spent the rest of the afternoon sleeping.

I start jogging down the narrow road. My ponytail swings back and forth along the back of my shoulders as I run. This country isn't one I've been to before. Gabe told me I had to be careful. Freaks are everywhere, he'd said. Don't I know it.

As I jog, I pass several stray animals, but they scamper off when they see me. A couple of cars pass by and one honks. I run until I find access to the public beach. The chain-link fence I come to is beat up, but once I walk through the gate, I find a nice beach. Not as nice as the ones back home, but it'll do. I run past an old fat man with a hairy white chest lying in the sand and dart along the shore. It feels good to run. I fill my lungs with the warm air and grin.

Gabe was right.

I did need a vacation.

I love my kids so much, and I can keep my darkness at bay. But sometimes…it's like I'm not me. I'm this other person. I stare at them with a stranger's eyes. Sometimes, I wish it were just me and Gabe. And those thoughts scare me. I wonder if the stranger within me will make that happen one day.

With a frown, I trot to a stop and bend over to catch my breath. Someone catcalls me. I jerk my head over to see that I'm standing in front of a dilapidated beach house. A man stands in the shadows under the porch.

"Oye mamita linda!" he hollers in a thick Spanish

accent and follows it with a whistle. He emerges from the shadows, puffing on a cigarette, and crudely grabs his crotch.

My chest aches from exertion and my calves are on fire. I look over my shoulder to see how far I've run. At least a mile…maybe two. I can't even see the hotel from this distance. Unease creeps up my spine.

"I don't speak Spanish," I yell back as I start hobbling away. My throat is on fire from thirst. I wish I'd have thought this out before I just ran off without my phone or telling my husband where I was going while in a foreign country.

"I speak English, pretty lady. Come a little closer. Are you thirsty? You look like you need a rest."

I turn to regard him. I *am* thirsty.

His eyes widen in shock when I start walking in his direction. When I'm close, he blatantly eye-fucks me. The guy is sort of cute, I guess. Probably late twenties. He needs a shower, but I don't think he has problems getting women.

"I'm Hannah," I tell him and give him a shy smile. "Staying over there with my husband."

He frowns and scratches his scruffy jaw with a finger while somehow managing to hold on to his cigarette. "Husband, eh?"

"Yep." I smile primly at him.

His gaze falls to my chest. I look down and frown to see two wet spots from where my nipples have leaked.

"Oh no," I groan. "Babies."

He takes a long drag of his cigarette while his eyes linger on my tits. "You look good, Mama."

I bask in his praise and bat my eyelashes at him. "Thanks. I thought you had something for me to drink."

He nods and licks his lips before tossing the cigarette into the sand. "I'm Pico." With a wave of his hand, he motions for me to follow him.

I wobble after him, wishing my calves didn't hurt so badly. I'll drink some water and then head back to the hotel. He slides open a dirty glass door at the back of the house. I follow him inside. One quick glance tells me this is an abandoned home. Trash litters the space and it reeks of feces.

"Where's the water?" I croak out.

The glass door slides shut behind me, and he stands between it and me. "There is no water."

I turn to him and frown. "Then why'd you invite me in?"

His brown eyes seem to darken and he lifts his T-shirt to reveal a gun tucked into his waistband. "You know why, white girl."

I curl up my lip. "Let me out of here, asshole."

A dark laugh rumbles from him. "No, cunt."

"My husband—"

He snorts and pulls the gun from his belt. "Your husband can't do shit."

I narrow my eyes at him and crack my neck. "I was going to say," I hiss, "that my husband will be angry if I kill you."

This sets him off because he attacks me. I'm tackled backward, and we land on a dirty mattress in the middle of the floor. He shoves the barrel of the gun under my chin as he uses his other hand to yank my pants down.

I don't fight or wiggle or anything.

I wait.

When he senses I'm not putting up a struggle, he glares at me. "What's wrong with you, puta? Are you fucking crazy?"

"You have no idea."

He snarls and roughly grabs me between my legs. His dirty finger pushes past my panties, seeking entrance. It burns when he gets it inside me. The gun feels cold against my jaw, but I'm not afraid. His zipper goes down, and he manages to take his cock out once he yanks his finger back out.

The wait is over.

He still holds the gun loosely in his one hand while the other is trying to help his cock thrust past my panties. I grip the key in my hand to form a weapon and I stab at his eyes.

Poke. Poke. Poke.

"Fuuuuck," he roars, abandoning his gun and me to cover his now bleeding face.

I grin as I shimmy my panties and pants back up my thighs. Sitting up on my knees, I grab his gun and point it at him. "You're going to regret ever waking up this morning."

He whimpers like a pussy. "Y-You fucking stabbed me in the eye!"

"Y-You tried to rape me," I mock and then cackle. "You messed up, buddy. You messed up real bad."

His cock is out and I laugh. Thin and the big bush of black hair surrounding it makes it seems shorter, too. No wonder he has to resort to rape. Nobody wants his tiny pecker. Poor fucker.

"Get naked."

He hisses. "What?"

"You wanna fuck? Let's fuck," I taunt.

"Fuck you, bitch."

I stand over him and kick his shoulder until he's on his back. With my gun pointed at his face, I snap at him, "I said get naked, asshole."

Terror flickers in his uninjured eye. With a shaking hand, he shoves his dirty underwear down and kicks away his jeans. Then, he pulls away his T-shirt. His chest is littered with poorly done tattoos, and it makes me giggle.

What a fucking loser.

"That's better," I coo. "Now, tell me how many girls you've raped."

He doesn't answer, so I fire a shot into his shoulder. The scream he lets out belongs to a teenaged girl, not a man.

"You psycho cunt!"

"How many girls have you raped?"

Snot dribbles down his lip and he shudders. "I don't know."

"Guess, asshole!"

He trembles. "Uh, six maybe?"

Six maybe?

Somehow I doubt that's true.

"Don't lie to me."

"Fuck, uh, fine. Maybe twenty or thirty."

I snort and straddle his waist. His one eye widens as he gapes at me in horror. But his stupid dick hardens beneath me. This asshole will always fuck with girls because he can't even manage to keep his cock soft when his eyeball is about to fall out and he has a bullet in his shoulder.

"Oh," I chide. "You're very bad, Pico."

He starts to cry, but I'll be damned if his cock doesn't throb beneath me.

"You need some relief, baby," I purr as I grip his jaw. "Need me to take care of that dick of yours?"

"Get away from me, puta!"

I laugh and obey the prick. For a moment. I find a discarded cola can and shove the barrel of the gun into the opening. The metal of the gun widens the opening. When I fire off another round, Pico screams. With the bottom of the can now bearing a hole, I push the gun through that hole too. Then, I regard him with an evil grin.

"Ready, Pico?"

"Get the fuck away from me," he hisses as he holds up his free hand, as if that'll protect him.

I pounce on him. When he tries to escape, I push the gun into his belly and fire off a shot that makes him scream louder than before. Both of his hands cover the hole that now spills with blood. While he's distracted, I grab his mediocre dick in my hand and shove the can down over his erection. And then I crush the aluminum can around him with my fist.

Screams.

One long continuous one followed by another

garbled one.

I sit on my butt and admire my handiwork. The head of his penis pokes out of the top of the can. Blood is everywhere.

"God, Pico, you're messy," I chide.

His hands try to pull the can away, but the sharp pieces of aluminum are digging into his sensitive flesh and preventing him from pulling it off. This makes me giggle.

"Y-You c-crazy f-f-fucking c-cunt," he chatters through his tears.

I stand and glower at him. "You should have just given me the water."

"Bitch!"

I smirk. "This bitch just fucked you up. By the way you're bleeding, I suspect you'll be dead before I even make it halfway back to the hotel. Goodbye, Pico."

He moans and groans, but I can tell he's weak. Blood spills from the hole in his stomach with every movement he makes. There's no way he'll live.

With a little wave at him, I tuck the gun into the back of my workout pants and tug the tank top over it to hide the bulge. As soon as I close the sliding glass door, I can no longer hear his cries over the waves. In the distance, the clouds are dark as a storm rolls in, making the water choppier.

I sprint the entire way back to the hotel with a giant smile on my face.

Pico, that sick rapist, really knew how to cheer a girl up.

Gabe

I WAKE TO THE SOUND OF A SHOWER RUNNING. IT'S dark out now and thunder rumbles nearby. I can't believe I slept for half the day. Now that we're here, away from my family, I can relax a bit. I don't have to watch Hannah's every move. We both needed the breather.

I slip out of bed and push my boxers down to join her in the shower. After a quick brush of my teeth, I find her under the spray, washing her hair.

"Hey, beautiful," I murmur as I draw her soapy body to me.

Her sudsy fingers find my shoulders and she beams at me. Clarity makes her eyes shimmer with light. She's fucking stunning. "Hey, handsome."

I tug her hair, so she looks up, and help her rinse the soap from it. Once she's clean, I grip her jaw and kiss her plump lips.

"What'd you do while I slept?"

My little liar bites on her lip. "Nothing much."

I snort. "Try again."

"Went for a run." Deception still flickers in her pretty eyes.

"Hannah," I warn, my fingers biting into her flesh. "Don't fucking lie to me."

Her fingers wrap around my cock, and she grips it hard. "I met a rapist."

I stiffen and glare at her. "Did he hurt you?"

A sexy smile plays on those dick sucking lips. "He tried."

I pull her to me and kiss the top of her head. She wraps her arms around my body. Her tits seem fuller than normal, smashed between us.

"What did you do?"

She looks up at me and wickedness gleams in her eyes. "I made sure he won't rape any more girls ever again."

My heart is hammering in my chest. I should yell at her for so many things. But all I can do is kiss her supple lips.

"My good girl," I praise. "God, I love you."

I grip her ass and lift her. She wraps her legs around my backside just as I push my cock into her wet cunt. I fuck her hard against the wall until she's screaming my name and clawing her nails down my shoulder. After I come deep inside her, I pull out of her and continue cleaning her perfect body. Small silvery stretch marks color the pale flesh near her hips, but I love the physical reminder of the children she grew inside her. *Our* children.

"What are we doing tonight?"

I cradle her face in my palm and grin at her. "I'm taking you to dinner. And then…"

"Dancing?"

I snort. "Better than that. We're going to do something fun after a little shopping."

"Oooh," she says, her eyes glimmering with mischief. "I'm excited."

"Wear black."

She arches a blonde brow at me. "This gets better and better."

"And maybe real shoes. Don't wear any fucking flip-flops."

"Yes, sir," she sasses and gives me a faux salute. "Anything else?"

I cup her pussy. "I'd like if this was easily accessible. Can you do that, sweet girl?"

She beams at me and nods.

"Good girl. Now get your ass ready so we can have some fun."

While Hannah blow dries her hair, I call Ren.

"How's my girl?" I ask in greeting when he answers.

"Good. What's up?"

I launch into what I need from him. It's asking a lot, I know. But, unlike his father, he doesn't argue. He simply takes note of my instructions and vows to fulfill my requests. Lastly, I give him the address before hanging up.

Just in time too.

Hannah shuts off the hairdryer and saunters into the room, with just a towel wrapped around her. I want to yank it off and nibble on her tits but I'm fucking starving for real food.

"Hurry and get dressed," I tell her as I pinch her ass through the towel. "We have reservations in twenty minutes."

She throws on a halter top black dress with a lovely open back and a plunging neckline. And like the obedient girl she is, she leaves off her panties and bra. I love that she's a stunner even without any makeup on. Then, she pulls on a tiny pair of white socks before slipping into a pink pair of Chucks. The shoes don't go with the dress, but she still looks fuck hot.

"Keep looking at me like you want to eat me and we may never leave this place," she says with a smirk.

I laugh and grab her hand. "Come on. We have shit to do."

Dinner was at the hotel and it was fucking delicious. They reserved a romantic table near the windows for us where we could watch the lightning. The storm seems to have stalled off in the distance and hasn't come ashore yet, but it won't be long before it reaches us. Once we've eaten, I pull up the address War found me, and we take a cab to the location, which is in a seedy part of town. The building is a pile of crap but it holds what we need.

"Let's do this, sweet girl," I instruct as I toss a wad of bills at the driver.

She climbs out, and the wind whips her dress

up. My sexy girl doesn't even bother with fighting to push it back down. With the moon shining on her blonde head and her round ass on full display, she's like some bad angel cast from heaven, luring men straight to hell. She simply struts up to the dilapidated building with her fine ass on display for me and the cabbie. And sure enough, when I glance at him, he's checking her out.

"Beat it," I snarl before trotting after her.

I tug the dress back down over her ass and guide her inside the building. It's dark and run-down inside, but a friendly guy greets us.

"Can I help you? Americans?" he chirps, his eyes nearly bugging out with dollar signs, like in the cartoons. He's a slimy bastard and greedy as hell. I can practically see him trying to calculate how much money he can make off us.

"Knives. I was told you had knives." I smile at him. "And other things."

His gaze flickers over to Hannah before he meets my stare. A question dances in his eyes. *Are you going to kill her?*

I smirk. *Eventually, I'm sure. But not today.* "My girl needs one too."

At this, he laughs. It's boisterous and over the top. "Oh, I have something to suit both your needs."

We follow him down the dark hallway toward the back. Hannah squeezes my hand. Not because she's nervous but because she's excited. My wife loves an adventure.

The room is brightly lit up with weapons lining the walls. Guns and knives and shit I wouldn't even know what to do with hang from hooks all over the place. I point at a backpack. "I want that."

The man pulls it down and sets it on a table. "You going to fill it up?"

Hannah glances over at me. "Please, Daddy?"

I snort and nod. "Fill it up, sweet girl."

The man, upon realizing that Hannah might be my daughter, takes a moment to check out her tits. So I walk up behind her and give them a squeeze. I meet his shocked stare and shrug. "She's got nice tits," I tell him and give one of her nipples a pinch. "Am I right?"

He nods and quickly picks up sharp long blade with an ivory handle. "This one is good for skinning."

She takes it from him and holds it up. "Too big."

I snag it from her and run my thumb along the blade. "Skinning you say?"

He nods again.

"I want it."

Hannah laughs and gives me a quick smile before

picking up a smaller knife. "I like this one."

"Bag it, baby."

The man seems pleased with our splurge. I toss in some handcuffs and a bundle of rope. He has everything we could possibly need—even a battery-operated light and a fifth of the country's best rum.

"Is that all?" the man questions, a weasel smile on his face.

I point behind him at a black-handled machete. "I want that too."

He obliges and then starts calculating my total. It's astronomical and obnoxious but I pull out a wad of bills and pay the man. After he counts it three times, he waves us toward the door.

"Thank you for doing business with us. Colombia welcomes you."

With the heavy-ass backpack slung over my shoulder, I take Hannah's hand and start walking toward our destination. I had War book us our hotel for a reason. It was close to where I wanted to go.

"A storm is coming," she says and points to the ocean where lightning illuminates the sky.

I squeeze her hand. "You have no idea, baby."

Under the moonlight with the wind kicking up her hair, I'm reminded of how much I love her. Hannah is my soulmate. My dark, dirty, hellion of a woman. It's been quite the ride to get us to this point. I don't want to lose her. Not now, not ever.

As we walk, I think about that emptiness I see in her eyes sometimes. I hate when that look presents itself in front of the children. They don't understand that their mother is sick. Toto takes it the hardest because she's older. She cries when Mommy is being cold toward her. I wish I could reach into Hannah's sick mind and patch up the hole that sometimes sucks all humanity from her.

And God how I've tried.

War and I have made her take every medicine we could get our hands on. Baylee has spent countless hours researching her daughter's mental illnesses. I've tried to preempt her moods and intervene. I'm good at distracting my wife but I never know how long it will work. And what happens when I'm *not* there to distract her? All it takes is one moment.

Guilt surges through me. I can't do that to my kids. I can't risk their lives. Their mother is unhinged and unstable. She's a vase full of cracks, and one day, water will gush out, drowning those she loves in the process. I've plugged those cracks, but I'm afraid I can't do that any longer.

There is only one way to save them.

"You're quiet," she murmurs.

I pull her into my arms and kiss her forehead. "I love you, baby. No matter what. Always and forever. And when this life is no longer ours, we'll rejoin in hell where nothing can stop us."

She tilts her chin up and beams at me. "My Hades."

I cup her jaw with my palm and run my thumb along her pink bottom lip. "My Persephone."

Her fingers grip the front of my shirt as she pulls me to her. Our mouths meet in a needy kiss. I'll never get enough of kissing her. If I had it my way, I'd keep kissing her until I'm old and on my deathbed. Then, I'd just kiss her until I take my last breath.

Something tells me it won't be so easy.

I slide my palm to her throat and run my fingertips along her vein. Her pulse is steady. Always so steady.

A crack of thunder makes us both jump. We pull away from our kiss, both of us panting for more.

"Come on," I bark. "We're almost there."

We pick up the pace down a desolate road that seems like it hardly ever sees any travelers. This is good because I don't need anyone seeing my ugly mug and screwing up my plans. The first raindrop that hits the back of my neck is cold. The second and third seem colder. When the heavens open up and rain down on us, I start running toward a chain-link fence. It's not electric, thank God, so I easily snap through the metal with the wire cutters I bought from the weasel guy earlier. I make a hole big enough for us to crawl through and send her through it first.

I should worry about dogs or some shit, but War has already given me the layout of the premises, and they don't have any vicious animals protecting the property. What they have is worse. They have big-ass Colombians with AK-47s strapped to their chests surrounding the perimeter. But, according to War, they don't have as many at night, and they mostly protect the front gate. Hannah and I should be good.

"What are we doing here?" she hisses. Her eyes flicker with excitement. My sweet girl is always down to be bad.

"You'll see," I tell her.

According to War's intel, one particular shipping container sees a lot of action. It isn't guarded at night, but during the day, people come and go. Even Brie's friend Vee and that fuckface Diego. War sent me some footage from when he hacked into their security system. What I've been looking for was last seen dragging a naked girl into the container months and months ago. He never came out, but she did. If he were dead, I doubt they would visit all the time, nor would it be so well guarded. And with what Brie told me about what happened to Vee when she went missing, I know it has to be *him*.

"This way," I bark out above the howling wind and pouring rain.

She runs behind me, along the outer perimeter. The shipping containers are stacked high and go on for as far as the eye can see. I finally find the one I'm looking for. It's older than the rest and hidden in the very back.

"What's inside?" she demands.

I smirk and use yet another tool I bought from that weasel. The fucker didn't even blink twice when I filled my bag with all this bizarre shit. But, he had all of said bizarre shit up for sale, so I guess it isn't that strange to a guy like him.

A bolt lock sits on the door handle. I unzip my backpack and pull out a crowbar. Once I wedge the metal in the lock, I throw all my weight down over and over again until the lock snaps. Hannah reaches forward and pulls the broken lock away.

I grab the machete and ready my weapon as I tug open the door with a noisy creak that is drowned out by the storm. My wife stands behind me, and together we walk inside. She manages to turn the light on, and soon the long narrow container is lit up. It reeks of feces and body odor and death. The emaciated form on the mattress rolls over and squints against the light.

"Is this…" Hannah trails off and takes a step forward, her wet shoes squeaking on the metal.

"Yep."

Her voice becomes a hiss. "Estebaaaaaaaaaaan."

IV | Hannah

HE PROMISED ME. NOT LONG AGO, AFTER WE found out what happened to Brie, I'd been enraged on her behalf. Having been a rape victim myself, it made me crazy furious that this Esteban dude fucked my husband's daughter. What's his is mine. Esteban raped what's mine. I told her I would kill him one day. Gabe promised me our chance would come. I never doubted my man for a second.

Esteban is naked and shivering. His black hair is long and hangs in his face. A black, coarse beard covers his cheeks and mouth.

"Help," he croaks out.

Gabe stays back, but I approach and set the lamp on the floor once I'm close. "Help with what, honey?"

I coo in a sugary sweet voice.

"Help me, please."

I look over my shoulder and Gabe stands with his back to the open container. His shoulders are broad and his chest heaves. My man is a barely contained storm. He wants to rage and make this man suffer for what he did to Brie. And what kind of wife would I be if I didn't help him?

"Can you move?" I question, my voice soft and concerned.

He tries to sit up but he's too weak. "I can't," he grunts. "You have to get me out of here."

I stroke his hair out of his face so I can look into the eyes of a sicko. "Who's done this to you?"

"Vienna, that fucking cunt. And her husband Diego Gomez. They're vicious. If they find you here, they'll have you killed," he hisses. "We have to go."

Gabe snorts and I suppress a grin.

"Shhh," I coo as I roll him to his back and straddle his stomach. My wet hair drips on his chest and he licks his lips. "Are you thirsty?"

He nods and stares up at me as if I'm an angel who's come to rescue him. *Hell's angel.* I grab a handful of my drenched hair and wring the water out over his mouth. A groan rumbles from him as he catches the wetness.

"Thank you," he murmurs.

I sit up on my knees and hold my dress out. "More? I can wring it out from my dress."

His gaze falls between my legs and his eyes widen. My pussy is naked and on full display. Since he doesn't answer, I wring my dress out into his open mouth. Then, I sit back down on his bare chest. My wet-from-the-rain pussy slides against his skin.

"W-Who are you people?" he demands, suspicion dancing in his eyes.

I rest my palms on his shoulders and rub against him. "I'm Hannah."

"Why are you here?" His jaw clenches as he glares at me. His fingers dig into my thighs over my dress. "Why the fuck are you here?"

Gabe grunts and stalks over to us, his heavy footsteps thundering in the metal tomb. He drops the bag beside Esteban and yanks his wrists above his head. "Don't talk to my fucking wife like that."

"D-Did Ricardo send you? Are you here to rape me too?" Esteban snarls up at my husband.

I laugh because it's fucking funny. This big, scary man is weak and helpless as Gabe cuffs him and then pins the cuffs with his knee. Esteban tears his gaze from Gabe to glower at me. Pleasure courses through me as I rub my pussy against his flesh. I scoot down until I meet the trail of hair below his belly button. His cock jolts and bounces against my ass crack through my dress.

"You like this," I accuse, a wicked smile on my face. Then, I flick my eyes up to Gabe. He watches me with narrowed eyes and a clenched jaw as I grind against this rapist's happy trail. With my thumb between my teeth, I lift my dress so my husband can see what I'm doing.

"Don't fuck him," Gabe orders.

I smirk. "I only fuck you."

"Damn right."

"You two are fucked up!" Esteban roars, his entire body coming alive with adrenaline. He must sense his fate. "Those cunts sent you, huh?"

"Shhh," I hiss as I rake my fingernails down his chest, breaking the skin as I go. "I want my knife, baby."

Gabe grunts and digs around in the bag. Once he hands me the small knife, he grips my wrist and yanks me until I fall into him. I kiss him hard with my thighs smashing Esteban's head. I'm getting into our kiss when Esteban bites the inside of my thigh. I screech and lift off from him. The knife clatters to the metal floor loudly.

"He bit me!"

Gabe snarls and grabs a handful of Esteban's hair. His wild eyes are on mine. "You okay, baby?"

I lift my dress and frown at the teeth marks. He didn't draw blood, but it still hurts. "Tape his mouth," I snap.

Gabe lets him go and finds the duct tape we bought earlier at the ghetto store. He rips off a giant strip and slaps it over Esteban's mouth. I stick my tongue out at the little biter and then straddle his face again so I can continue kissing my man. Esteban's hot breath comes out hard through his nose and it tickles my sensitive flesh. A tiny moan escapes me.

"You're such a dirty girl," Gabe mutters against my mouth as he grabs my ass through my wet dress. "What are you doing under there?"

I rub myself against Esteban's nose and jolt when the tip of it touches my clit. "Nothing."

"Little liar," Gabe says with a grin. "Show me. Take this shit off."

I match his wicked smile and peel off my soaked dress. It hits the metal floor with a slap. Gabe and I look between us. Esteban's wild eyes are staring up at us as if we're crazy, his chest heaving.

Maybe we are.

Gabe's eyes find mine as he grabs my hips. He urges me closer to him. Esteban's nose pokes inside me and it feels good. My eyes roll back when his hot breath rushes inside me.

"Oh!" I cry out.

Esteban jolts from beneath me as he struggles to breathe. Gabe pins my hips so that I can't move anywhere.

"Touch your clit, baby," Gabe instructs.

I reach down and rub at my sensitive bundle of nerves. With Esteban fighting for breath inside me and his face moving back and forth, I'm overcome with a delicious sensation. Gabe's mouth finds mine and he kisses me hard. I close my eyes and give into the wonderful feelings surging through me. Esteban stills just as I climax. I shudder wildly. The moment Gabe lets me go, I lift up to let my little biter friend have some air.

He inhales a deep breath and then breathes so heavily, I wonder if he'll hyperventilate.

"Hold his hands." Gabe's eyes are nearly black with fury and madness. I fucking love that look in his eyes.

I take Esteban's wrists and hold them down. Not that he's going anywhere anyway. His body is weak and his eyes are barely open. Gabe stands and walks off. I stroke Esteban's hair from his eyes.

"Awww," I coo. "You okay, sweetie?"

Esteban's eyes widen for a minute and then he shakes his head.

I tug at his facial hair. "You survived. Just like Gabe's daughter did when you drugged and raped her multiple times."

He closes his eyes as realization sets in.

I give his cheek a slap. "Open up, honey. The sins of your past have come back to haunt you."

His dark eyes are wild as they glare up at me. Despite his weak body, fire still burns inside him. Some monsters don't die easily.

"What are we doing?" I question as I look over my shoulder at Gabe.

He runs his fingers through his dripping hair and levels me with a hard gaze. "I want to punish him for everything he did to her but I'm so pissed I can't think straight."

I beam at my husband. "That's why you have me." I pick up the knife and turn back to Esteban. He brings his cuffed hands in front of him and attempts to push me away but he's weak. I use my knee to pin his cuffed arms against his lower belly. Then, I wiggle the knife at him.

"Ready, Esteban? Ready to tell Gabriella you're sorry?" I scream, my spittle spraying him.

He starts shaking his head, but I ignore him as

I begin carving his apology into his flesh. The garbled and choked sounds he makes fuel my adrenaline. When I finish, I shake away my daze and find Gabe kneeling beside me, his attention fully on me. A beautiful smile adorns his handsome face.

"I'm sorry for raping you, Gabriella," Gabe says as he reads my bloody artwork.

Esteban is breathing heavily, his eyes dilated. Sweat pours from his face. But it's the blood rushing down the sides of his abdomen that is so pretty. Red against his pale flesh. I drop my knife to the side and rub my palms through the blood. It smears, and new blood rushes out in its wake.

Turning my head to regard Gabe, I catch his gaze before rubbing the blood all over my breasts and belly. Gabe growls and licks his lips.

"You're so fucking hot, baby," he utters in a soft, deadly voice. "I want to fuck your pretty little ass."

I rub my bare bottom against Esteban's sweaty lower stomach. "So do it."

"That dickhead will probably like it," he snarls.

My gaze drifts back to Esteban's. "We'll punish him if he does."

Gabe stands and kicks off his shoes. He tugs his shirt off and his pants drop to the floor. My man is absolutely gorgeous in all of his naked, masculine glory. And, dear God, his cock is amazing.

"Give me your ass, Hannah," he orders as he kneels behind me.

I rest my forearms on Esteban's chest as I straddle his hips. My ass pokes in the air, ready for my man. When I feel his cold palm on my lower back, I let out a breath of anticipation. Esteban is staring at me with hate in his eyes. I expect him to try to shove me away, but he's too weak and his hands remain cuffed, resting on his lower belly.

"Is your pussy wet, baby?" Gabe questions as the tip of his cock rubs against my clit.

"Mmm-hmmm."

"It better be," he bellows. "If you want lube for your ass, your cunt better provide it."

His words turn me on, and a shiver ripples through me. "I'm so wet."

As if to test me, he pushes his cock inside of me. My body is soaked and easily accepts his thickness. He drives into me with a few thunderous thrusts. When he pulls all the way out, I know where he'll go next. The moment he pushes against the tight hole of my ass, I cry out. He's so big, but I love when he stretches me wide open and threatens to tear me apart. Inch by inch, he drives into me until he's completely buried.

"Touch yourself," Gabe orders, his cock throbbing but unmoving inside me.

I reach between my legs and brush against Esteban's bound hands before I find my clit. The moment I find the sweet spot, I let out a whimper of pleasure. Gabe takes this as his moment to start pounding into me. The faster he goes, the faster I move my fingers. My eyes lock on Esteban's. His dark eyes are positively manic. And when I tear my gaze from his to look between us, I can see how turned on he is, despite his helpless state. His cock jolts and his bound hands reach for it.

"He likes this," I breathe.

Gabe groans and thrusts almost painfully into my ass. I'm turned on as I touch myself and watch this sick fuck attempt to fondle himself. A scream escapes me when Gabe grabs a handful of my hair and yanks me all the way upright. He glares over my shoulder to see what Esteban is up to. Then, his mouth attacks mine. The pleasure of having him buried deep in my ass, coupled with how I'm rubbing my clit, has me crashing into oblivion. A long moan erupts into Gabe's mouth as I lose myself to ecstasy. The moment I begin to shudder, Gabe explodes with his orgasm inside my ass. Esteban groans loudly enough to steal me from my husband's kiss. I look down in time to see his semen spurt up his belly.

"Oh, no," I chide. "Bad boy wasn't supposed to do that."

Gabe snarls when he slides out of my ass. He storms over to his clothes and throws his jeans back on. Then, he grabs me by the elbow and jerks me up to my feet. My legs still quiver from my orgasm, and I nearly collapse.

"I want to hear his screams. Rip the tape off his mouth, baby," he orders as he releases me. "But I want to see your sexy naked body, so don't dress yet. I want to watch you while my cum leaks out of your ass."

I grin at him as I bend over to remove the tape. His cum does run out of me and down my thighs. My husband is so dirty. I fucking love it.

Esteban doesn't make a sound when I rip off the tape but the moment he realizes it's gone, he starts babbling.

"M-Money. Whatever you want. I'll give it to you," he murmurs, his voice weak and breathless. His eyes are on mine, as if I have the ability to sway Gabe's mind on what he plans to do.

"We don't want money. We want your life," I tell him simply.

"P-Please…"

I kneel beside him and swipe his sweaty hair from his eyes. "Stop begging. Bad guys don't beg. They take their punishment and they die like the motherfucking villains they are. Got it, Esteban? Stop acting like a pussy and take it like a man."

His eyes turn hard. "Just cut my throat."

I pick up my knife and tease his neck with it. "That would be too easy, baby doll. I think my husband wants your dick—and not in a sexual way."

Esteban groans as a tear leaks from the corner of his eye.

"And I think you owe us a tongue. Gabe is quite disturbed about the fact that you took that sweet little girl's tongue," I tell him as I run my bloody finger over his bottom lip. "It takes a lot to disturb my husband. But late at night, he asks me about it. We discuss how painful that must have been for that little girl. She's big now, though. And even without a tongue, she somehow still found love with my brother. They kiss. I've seen pictures on his Facebook. You could probably kiss without your tongue too." I drag my knife along his torn chest to his belly button. I skim over his handcuffed hands, letting the blade hit the metal with a clink before I poke his flaccid dripping cock. "But can you fuck without your cock?"

He attempts to steal the knife, but I hold it away, laughing. "Not so fast, bud."

Gabe drops to his knees on the other side of Esteban and cups my cheek with his hand. "You're so beautiful when you're free. I wish I could free you forever."

I frown and regard his sad eyes for a moment. "I'm free when I'm with you."

His gaze darkens as his palm slides to my throat. "You think so?"

My fingers grip his wrist and I smile at him. "I know so."

The sadness seems to dissipate and determination sets in. I love how fierce my man is. "I'm going to pry his mouth open and you take his tongue. For Luci," Gabe snarls, his glare firm.

"My pleasure, baby," I tell him.

It's a struggle, but my husband is much stronger than the weak man in captivity. He manages to pry his mouth open. And with glee, I saw right through the muscle until I free Esteban of his tongue. He gurgles and blood spurts from his mouth.

I grip Gabe's bearded face with my bloody fingers and motion my head toward Esteban's lower region. "Now, for Brie."

He nods and scoots farther down. I straddle

Esteban's chest and hold his face in my palms. The life is draining from his eyes as the blood gushes from his mouth. He chokes and spits. His tongue sits discarded beside his head, and the sight of it makes me wonder what happened to Luci's. Did he just throw it somewhere?

"You're dying, pig," I whisper and kiss his nose that smells like me. "Accept it, baby."

Tears stream down his cheeks, and then an unholy scream makes it past the blood in his throat as Gabe delivers his final vengeance. The sound of his flesh tearing is sickening and unlike anything I've ever heard before. Something hot sprays against my bare back and I shiver. It's done. Esteban's been robbed just like he robbed so many before him. Gabe is the dark avenging angel straight from the catacombs of hell tasked with sending the demon to meet his maker. An eternity of suffering for his sins. I hug the bloody dying man as he quickly slips from our world into the next. His entire body spasms until it doesn't move anymore. The rise and fall of his chest stops. The gurgling and choking is silenced.

"Good boy," I say with a grin and kiss his cheek before I stand. My gaze skims to where Esteban's cock once was. Blood is everywhere. What a mess.

Gabe glares down at him, but the rage is

calming. I wrap my arms around him and rest my cheek to his bare chest.

"We should get back soon. It's late," I tell him with a yawn. "If we want to make the buffet breakfast in the morning, I need sleep."

His strong hand finds my throat and he glares down at me. The wild look in his eyes is one I don't recognize. Monstrous. Cold. Not my husband. "Who said we were leaving?" He squeezes hard enough to cut off my air supply. I start to black out.

This is it. He's made his decision to end me once and for all.

Black.

Black.

Silence.

When I reopen my eyes, I realize the cold rain hitting my naked flesh is what woke me. Gabe carries me through the storm past the rows of containers and back toward the fence. I wrap my arm around his neck and bury my face into his flesh.

"I love you," I croak, my voice hoarse from his choking.

He kisses the top of my head as a low growl escapes him. "I love you too, baby."

Maybe he doesn't have it in his heart to kill me.

At least for now…

V | Gabe

One month later...

I'M STARING UP AT THE CEILING WITH MY ENTIRE life in my arms. Hannah is on one side of me with our son sleeping between us. Toto is curled up against my side with her small arm slung across my middle. Everyone is asleep. It's been a few weeks since we came back from our "vacation" where we ended that sicko. And it's as if my entire little family knows our world is about to dramatically shift. We all cling together in these moments.

It fucking kills me.

My heart breaks for them.

Their mother is dangerous. I'd hoped the trip would sort her out. If anything, it only made her

57

more blood thirsty. The feral look in her eyes—that same manic one from the shipping container—hasn't dissipated. I can't leave her alone with the children. I'm scared to fucking death I'm going to wake up to another bloodbath, but this one will steal my soul.

I reach over and stroke her hair. So soft and silky. How can I ever let her go? Truth is, I can't. But I have to fix this. Everyone in my family is relying on me.

Thank God I have Ren on my side.

He's been helping me plan.

Tomorrow night, on the eve of his wedding to my daughter, is when we will carry it out. Hannah can't go to the wedding anyway because my Brie loathes her. It has to be done then.

Land stirs, so I scoop him up and lay him across my chest. I stroke his dark hair before kissing the top of his head. Babies have made me soft. Ever since Brie came into my life, I've become weaker. My children have made me this way. Love makes you weak. So fucking weak. But, fuck, if I don't like being weak from it.

Hannah lifts her hand and strokes our son's back before whispering. "He's so cute."

I smile and turn to see her eyes softer than usual. The darkness is gone as love shines through. I wish to hell I knew how to keep that look in her eyes.

"Because he looks like me," I tell her in a smug tone.

She laughs, which makes Land jump but not wake up. "Sometimes I wish you wouldn't have gotten fixed. We could have more."

My chest aches. I'd love to have more children. But the fact is, we can't. Not with her mental health situation. We've tried every drug imaginable. There is no bringing light to her darkness. It's just who she is. War is still in denial, but I've come to peace with it. There's no fixing her, unfortunately.

Death is the only way out of her darkness.

"Come on," I tell her, changing the subject. "Let's take the kids to the beach today. One last family day."

She tenses. "One *last* family day?"

"Before all this wedding stuff takes over our lives starting this evening. Toto has to try on her flower girl dress. I have to pick up my tux. Brie wants me to come see the babies and have dinner with them before the rehearsal. Just a lot going on," I tell her softly.

"I wish Ren would just get over it and let me come," she huffs.

"It's not Ren who has the problem, baby."

"It was an accident." Her response to killing Alejandra is always the same. But since it isn't true, nobody believes her. Especially not Brie.

"I know," I lie, indulging her. "They'll come around eventually and I'll make sure to get pictures for you."

Satisfied, she curls against me and kisses my cheek. "Let's sleep for a little while longer. The beach will wait for us."

Toto squeals as Hannah chases her along the shore. Land sleeps sprawled next to me on our blanket under the umbrella. My attention never leaves my girls. All it would take is one second. My phone buzzes, and I quickly read the message.

Ren: Done. All ready. All you have to do is get her here. Then this nightmare will be over.

I bristle at his abrupt tone. His sister, my wife, is not a nightmare. She's troubled. I hate that I have to do this to her. I scrub my face and scan the beach for her. Her eyes are on mine as she walks hand in hand with Toto. I grin and wave at her. She smiles back. Today she wears a skimpy black bikini that makes my cock hard. I'm going to miss moments like these after tomorrow.

Me: I'll take the kids to your parents tonight.

Give me more time with her. Then, I'll bring her.

He responds right back.

Ren: Fine, but I want it done before the wedding. Consider it your gift to your daughter.

I grumble but type out my reply.

Me: Done.

After I delete all the messages, I tuck my phone away in the beach bag. Land wakes and starts squirming.

"Hey, baby boy," I coo and kiss his belly through his onesie. "Let's go play with Mommy and your sister. Looks like our time is limited."

He grunts and waves his fist at me as if he's trying to argue. If there were any other way, I'd be arguing too. But there's not. This is it. This is the end, baby.

I scoop him into my arms and stand. When Toto sees me, she squeals and runs for me. Hannah's smile is brighter than the sun beaming down on us.

Why can't all days be like this one?

"A date the night before the wedding?" Baylee

grumbles as she rocks Land in her arms. "I still have to cut up all that fruit and a mountain of vegetables for the reception. How am I supposed to do that if I have to babysit?"

Calder saunters in with his no-tongue girlfriend on his heels. That kid and I don't like each other, but at least he loves my children. He takes Land from his mother while Luciana signs to her.

"We can babysit," Calder translates. "Or we can cut vegetables. It's fine."

Hannah remains silent as she refuses to speak to her mother. They talk sometimes about the kids, but the conversation is usually strained. Sometimes, like tonight, they don't speak at all. I pull her to my side and thank Calder. "We *need* this."

Our eyes meet, and he gives me a clipped nod. It makes me wonder if Ren's confided in him about what we have planned. Wouldn't surprise me. I am shocked, though, that he doesn't try to stop me. The only one who would try would probably be Baylee. For Hannah's biggest thorn, she's always been the fiercest about protecting her.

Not this time, Baylee.

The plan is in motion, and your fucking boys are going to help me.

"Let me tell Toto bye and then we'll leave," I grit

out as I release Hannah to go hunt for my daughter. I find her in War's office, sitting in his lap. He's turned on a computer game for her and only winces a little bit when she beats on his keyboard.

"We're about to head out," I tell him as I enter the office.

Toto ignores me, so I ruffle her hair and kiss the top of her head. "Bye, baby girl."

"Bye, Daddy," she chirps and bangs her fist again.

"How are the new meds?" War questions.

I meet his steely gaze and shrug. "Same as the others. Fucking worthless."

His lips press into a firm line. "I'll keep trying."

"Soon it won't matter."

Hard blue eyes dart to mine and his jaw clenches. "I told you I didn't want the specifics."

I snort. "Well, neither do I but here we fucking are."

Toto is oblivious as she plays her game. Meanwhile, War pinches the bridge of his nose, and I pace his office.

"It's our only option," I mutter. "If there were any other way, you know I'd be up for it." I swallow and pat Toto's head. "I can't lose these kids."

Understanding washes over him and he nods. "I know. I just..." His jaw clenches again. "I just don't want to know about it. It hurts too fucking much. Because in order to protect *your* kids, we have to hurt *mine.*"

I place my hands on my hips and give him a hard stare. "This protects your other children as well, you know. You and Baylee too."

He closes his eyes, and a ragged breath escapes him. "I know, but I don't like it."

"Neither will she."

"Where are we going?" Hannah asks from the passenger seat.

Tonight, she looks killer in a pale blue summer dress that shows off her toned thighs. I'm dying to mark them up with my teeth. I reach over to squeeze her leg and then run my pinky under her dress and along the seam of her panties.

"Somewhere special."

She smiles, and it's so beautiful I almost change my mind. For a split second, I almost turn the car the fuck around. But when her blue eyes flicker with that ever-present darkness, I'm reminded that this ends tonight.

"Would you ever kill me?" I ask as I tease her flesh while I drive.

She's quiet but manages to give me a shrug.

I give her skin a little pop. "I asked you a yes or no question, baby."

Her glare snaps to mine. "If I had to, then yes."

"The things we do for love," I say softly.

The two-hour drive is intense. With every passing mile, I feel a part of my soul chipping away. And she must sense the foreboding because she's tense. I glance over and catch her chewing on her fingernail.

I need to calm her down.

To ease her nerves.

I drive until I find a road that's lined with thick trees on either side. When I shut off the car, she stiffens.

"Is this the part where you kill your wife?" she demands, her small hands fisted.

"Don't be fucking ridiculous," I snap.

"Then what?"

I reach up and pinch her tit through her dress. "Get your skinny ass over here."

Her shoulders relax. "You just want to fuck?"

"I always want to fuck you."

A small laugh escapes her as she climbs over the center console into my lap. Our mouths connect in a needy kiss as she scrambles to pull my hard cock from my jeans. I barely mange to pull her panties to the side before she's guiding me inside her. Her body slides down my length and she pulls away to stare at me. I grip her hip with one hand to urge her body to move but use my other hand to stroke her soft blonde hair.

She's mine.

Ever since the day I knew she existed in her mother's belly.

"I love you," I tell her, my tone fierce. "No matter what."

She chews on her bottom lip and nods. Fat, genuine-as-fuck tears well in her pretty blue eyes. My girl is intuitive. Always has been. She knows that life as we've known it ends tonight.

"I'm sorry," she chokes out as her lips attack mine. "I'm sorry I can't be better for you."

I drown out her stupid words by kissing her deeply. Her seated on my cock with her tongue in my mouth is where she belongs. I slip my thumb to her front and rub it against her clit through her panties.

"Gabe," she moans as her head tilts back in pleasure.

"That's it, sweet girl," I growl. "Come all over my big dick. Get me messy, baby."

I lean forward and bite her tit through her dress. She trembles as her fingers clutch my hair. All it takes is a moment more of me rubbing her needy pussy before she's climaxing with my name on her lips as though it's a curse.

I've always been her curse.

The black fucking plague.

Hannah's own little nightmare.

I bury my face against her tits as my orgasm explodes from me. I'm in heaven when her body is wrapped around my cock. All the bad in our life feels good for just one moment. I can forget it all and pretend we're okay. But as soon as my seed trickles back out of her body, awareness settles over me.

No more putting this off.

I have to drive her to the place that she'll never leave.

VI | Hannah

THE END IS NEAR. I CAN FEEL IT. DESPITE HIS denial, a sense of foreboding has washed over me. Finality. I'm perceptive enough to know when my husband's behavior changes. He's not the loving, doting husband he usually is.

He's hard.

His jaw is clenched and he's white-knuckling the steering wheel.

Poised and ready to kill.

I should be worried or panicking but I'm not. I know something is wrong with me. We both know this. If I keep barreling down this path called Life, I'm going to eventually crush the ones I love. The thought of hurting my children sickens me. I love them as much as I love Gabe. And if I were to hurt them, he'd never forgive me.

It's better this way.

Tears swim in my vision, and I quickly blink them away.

I'm a strong woman. I can handle this.

My mind begins to wander. How will he kill me? With a rope around my throat? I'd rather it be his strong hand. With a knife tearing open my flesh like we cut up Esteban? I hope he does it slow so I can savor his beauty while my life bleeds out. Shot to the head? As long as he's holding me when I go, I'm okay with that.

A quiver shakes through me.

I don't want to die.

I'm too young and I have too much love to give. Fighting my demons is a daily battle, but it's always worth it because my prize is my family. Gabe and Toto and Land need me. Only I know how to cut up Toto's apples the way she likes them. It's only me who knows that when you brush your thumb along Land's brow after he eats, he falls asleep quicker. And nobody but me knows that when you cradle Gabe against your breast, his breathing evens out and all the stress leaves his body—that he snores ever so softly, and that's how you know he's fully at peace.

It's the little things.

They're mine to love and take care of.

I shouldn't be taken away from them.

"Almost there," Gabe says in a husky tone. He won't look at me, which crushes a deep piece of my soul.

I squint in the darkness as we drive slowly down a winding road lined with trees. The speed limit said forty miles per hour, and yet he's dipping way below. He doesn't want to do this. I don't want him to either.

"Gabe," I choke out, my tears falling freely now.

"Shhh," he murmurs and takes my hand. "It'll all be over soon."

I start to sob. My chest feels as though it's going to explode. The love is all inside. It's locked up but it seeps out through my cracks. This love belongs to him and our babies. One drip at a time might be all they get, but it's theirs. And there is so much more where that love came from. I just don't know how to make the holes bigger.

He turns down a gravel driveway that leads to a pretty house with many windows. On the side of the yard is a newly built swing set. It appears to be a perfect home for a family. The thought makes me cry harder. But when I see my brother Ren's truck, my blood runs cold.

That fucking traitor.

Of course, Ren would want to help kill me. He'd do it himself if he had his way. Hell, that may be why he's here. Maybe Gabe knew he wouldn't be able to do it by himself.

"Hannah," Gabe mutters before turning his head to frown at me. "I love you."

I swallow. "I love you too."

"If there were any other way..." he trails off. His brows pinch together as pain flickers in his eyes. He tugs my hand to pull me closer. Then, his other hand is in my hair. I let out a sad moan when his lips press to mine. Soft and sweet. He deepens the kiss, and I try to memorize the taste of his tongue. His manly scent that comforts me. The way his love follows him around like a warm fog always blanketing me.

"Promise me something," I whisper against his lips. "Promise me *you'll* do it. Don't let Ren be the one to kill me. I want it to be you."

A growl rumbles from him. "Hannah..."

"But first"—I whimper as I pull away to regard his handsome face. I free my hand from his and touch his wiry beard—"First, you have to catch me."

His brown eyes flare to life with need and desire and love and animalistic fury all swirled into one storm. A storm only I can create. I don't give him time to react before I yank on the handle and throw myself out of the car. I abandon my flip-flops in the car as I take off running through the soft grass toward the tree line.

"HANNAH!" he roars from behind me as he climbs out of the car.

I don't look back.

I just run.

He's going to catch me.

He always does.

My hair flies out behind me as I bolt. The air is fairly warm tonight. It's a beautiful night to die. His heavy footsteps thud behind me, so I pick up my pace. The moment I enter the woods, I know it by the bite of the underbrush on my bare feet. Twigs and pinecones and thorny plants tear at my soles, but they don't stop me.

I run and run and run.

His heavy breathing grows closer. I bet if I were to turn around, he'd be just a few feet away. So I don't turn around. I can't afford one small mistake. My tears seem like a permanent fixation on my cheeks. I know that I'll die with those tearstains on my cheeks. I just hope I also die with his face being the last thing I see. Fingers brush against the back of my dress, and I screech. I run faster.

Just not fast enough.

With a grunt from him, he tackles me to the forest floor. The crash and fall is brutal. Sticks poke at me and thorns seem to stab at me from every direction. His weight crushes me to the earth. My husband easily wrangles my wrists behind my back as he presses his hard body against me. We're both breathing heavily, so neither of us speaks at first.

This is it.

All over now.

"Why'd you run, sweet girl?"

I swallow down my emotion. "So you'd catch me one last time."

His lips press to my cheek as he seeks my mouth from behind. I turn my head to steal one last kiss. But the kiss isn't enough for either of us. He rips my dress up over my ass and yanks my panties down my thighs. Then, he struggles with his pants until his hot cock is freed and pressing against me. He works his knee between mine. When I try to move my wrists, he tightens the grip.

"I'll never get tired of fucking you, wild woman," he says as he guides his cock to my opening. I'm slick and hot for him. When he pushes into my pussy, I cry out in need. With one hard thrust, he drives all the way into me.

Pain assaults me from every direction, but the pleasure always supersedes the pain. I'd take all the pain as long as Gabe was the one doling it out. He fucks me hard against the brush. He utters beautiful words about love and family and destiny the whole time. I get lost in them—in him—and unravel with a scream. A grunt and then a growl escape him before he's gushing inside of me. When we're no longer moving, but he's still buried deep inside me, I let out the breath I'd been holding.

"I'm ready," I tell him, my voice quivering slightly.

"Ready for what?"

"This is the end, baby. Kill me, so I don't kill them." My voice cracks. "Or you."

He slides out of me and his cum leaks out. I'm then released as he pulls his pants back up. "Come here."

I'm unable to move, so he tugs my panties into place before hooking his arm around my waist to haul me to my feet. I lean my back against his chest in an effort to steal another moment with him. His palm slides up to grip my tit through my dress as his mouth finds my ear. A shiver ripples through me at having his hot breath there.

Soon, I'll never feel his hot breath again.

It'll be so cold without him.

"I love you," he assures me again.

A crunch in the woods jerks my attention toward the direction we came from. Not even thirty feet away, a giant shadowy figure stalks toward us. Fear races down my spine until I catch a glimpse of the familiar face. More of my love seeps out through my stupid cracks.

"Did you really have to do that when I'm within shouting distance?" Ren asks.

My eyes fall to the hammer in his grip. I freeze in Gabe's arms. A hammer? Fucking really?

"J-Just shoot me," I beg, tears once again hot in my eyes. "Don't bludgeon me to death!"

Ren snorts and shakes his head. "If it were my way, big sis, I'd have shot your ass a long time ago." The hate in his eyes doesn't mask the love he still harbors, though. I see it. A slight flicker of light amidst his dark rage.

"I'm sorry," I choke out. I truly am sorry for what became of my relationship with my brother.

"Not sorry enough," he snarls as he storms toward us. He has something in his other hand, but I'm not able to make out what it is because in the next second, everything turns black.

Black.

Black.

Cold.

"I love you, sweet girl."

And then nothing.

VII | Gabe

MY DAUGHTER IS GETTING MARRIED. AGAIN. THE girl is barely twenty years old and she's on her second marriage. I never knew the first guy, but this guy is okay. He's a product of Baylee, so how could he not be?

I let my gaze drift over to where Baylee is fussing over the dark purple bow on Toto's white dress. The woman I once loved is still just as beautiful as she was when I had her for the very first time. Fuck, she might even be more beautiful. Age has done her well. A spitting fucking image of her mother, Lynn. The teal-colored dress she's wearing hugs her body in all the right ways, accentuating the globes of her breasts. Hannah would have been so jealous of her mother had she been able to be here today for this wedding.

Guilt and heartache have my jaw clenching.

Last night was the worst night of my life.

I'm hollow now.

"He'll take care of her," War assures me as he clutches my shoulder in a supportive way. Twenty years ago I'd have murdered him for merely looking at me. And yet, here we are. Friends of sorts. I'm sure Baylee is proud.

I smirk and shrug. "Brie is a tough cookie. If he does her wrong, she has enough of her daddy in her to make sure it doesn't happen again."

War chuckles and shifts their baby Mason to his other hip. "You're right about that."

Toto squeals and runs over to me. I scoop her into my arms and plant a kiss on her soft cheek. "You'll always stay my baby girl, huh? You're never going to get married."

"Daddy's baby," she agrees, her brown eyes wide and happy.

My heart swells when she nuzzles against me and hugs me with her small arms. I'm grinning like a fool when my gaze meets Baylee's. Normally, she glares at me. Cold stares filled with hate.

But not today.

Today, Baylee regards me like she did long ago,

back when I was someone in her life who she cared for. Her eyes shine with love for my daughter, and a smile plays at her lips. It hurts me how fucking much she and Hannah resemble each other.

"How much longer?" I question.

She reaches forward and adjusts the boutonniere on my lapel, which Toto jostled. "Ren and Calder are finishing up. Luci's in with Brie, making sure her makeup is just right. I think we're ready to begin."

"Where are the twins?" I question.

She pulls a baby monitor from her clutch and waves it at me. "Same place as Land. Napping in the church nursery. Brie wanted them in the wedding, but they've been extra fussy lately so she decided to let them sleep."

"Is the devil even allowed in church?" Calder questions with a laugh from behind me. "Shouldn't your skin be sizzling or some shit?"

"Calder!" Baylee chides. "Don't say 'shit' in church. I can't take you anywhere."

I snort and eyeball the Justin Bieber looking kid with a raised eyebrow. "The devil was an angel once." That comment earns me an eye roll from both him and Baylee, which has me chuckling.

I sober up, though, when Ren walks out and stands beside his brother. Had I not had his help last night, I'm not sure where my life would have ended up. I'll owe him that debt until the day I can repay him. But now he's about to vow to take care of my Brie baby for the rest of his life. For that, I'll never be able to repay him.

"I'm counting on you," I tell him as I reach out to shake his hand.

He gives me a firm shake. The kid is a man now. He'll fuck up anyone who even looks at my daughter wrong. I'm thankful she has a built-in bodyguard for her and the twins.

"So is she," he replies. "I love her and I'm going to spend the rest of my life showing her that."

"You better," I say with a grin. "I know where you live. And you know what I can do if you slack off. Don't fucking slack off."

"Gabriel Sharpe!" Baylee hisses. "Church. Stop trying to get us kicked out."

Calder starts laughing, but Ren starts shoving him down the aisle in a playful brotherly way. My heart rate picks up. I can't wait to see my daughter all dressed up and ready to marry a McPherson.

"You asleep, sweet girl?" I coo to Toto.

She lifts her head and beams at me. "I big girl. No nap."

War ruffles her hair before taking Baylee's hand.

Together, the two of them along with their small son, walk down the aisle and find a seat.

I kneel down and set Toto to her feet. "Where's your basket?"

She points over to the table but then regards me with a frown. "Mommy?"

A pang of guilt slices through me. "Mommy's sleeping," I lie.

"Nap like baby?"

I hug her to me and kiss her soft blonde hair. "Yep. Now go get your basket."

She runs off just as the music starts playing. By the time she returns, the door down the hallway opens. Luci steps out wearing a knee-length dark purple, almost black, dress. Her long black hair has been pulled up in a fancy style on top of her head. The engagement ring Calder gave her glimmers in the light. She smiles broadly when she sees me. Luci and I hit it off pretty easily. For being a mute, the girl has a lot to say. But if she texts me one more Justin Bieber meme… Sometimes I regret bringing her that bastard's tongue as a vacation souvenir because apparently that means we're best goddamned friends now.

"Luci!" Toto shrieks and runs over to her, losing half her flower petals along the way.

The pretty Colombian woman squats to hug my daughter. It warms my once-cold heart. She signs to Toto. Toto sets her basket down and signs *I love you,* which is something Calder has been teaching her. Luci grins and signs it back before kissing her on the forehead. She stands and looks back in the room. Her hands do some fancy motions. Then I hear my other daughter.

"I'm too big for this dress," Brie pouts.

As I stalk toward the room where I can hear her mumbling to herself, I can't help but smile. Inside, I find an angel. *My* angel. A lump forms in my throat upon seeing my beautiful girl. She looks so much like Alejandra, it's dizzying. Her mother would be so proud of the woman she's grown into.

"Daddy," she chokes out.

"You look gorgeous, Brie baby. Fucking gorgeous."

A laugh escapes her. "I've gained weight since I bought the dress. I look terrible."

At this, I raise an eyebrow. "You could never look terrible. Even if you tried."

Her smile is radiant. "Ren says the same thing. You both are strange."

"*Love* is strange."

When I start humming her favorite *Dirty*

Dancing song, she giggles just like she used to when she was a kid.

"Sylvia?" I ask with a grin and hold out my hand.

"Yes, Mickey?"

I tug her to me, and she steps on my fancy shoes. While I hum the song "Love is Strange," we dance around the small dressing room, until she begins humming the melody along with me. She rests her head against my chest. I dance with my daughter, enjoying the moment, until Luci knocks on the door, motioning to us that it is time for us to go with her.

Leaning forward, I press a kiss to Brie's forehead and then I offer her my arm. She hooks her arm in mine, and I walk my daughter out to marry her off to her husband. I may be giving her away, but she'll always be my baby.

The ceremony is a blur.

Two kids who have been through so fucking much vowing to love each other till the end. It's beautiful, and I wish Hannah could have seen it. My heart is heavy but it was the right thing to do. The only way.

The vows. The rings. The kiss.

It's all a haze.

Regret and sadness try to steal me from the moment. It almost does. But then these two strong kids raise their conjoined hands as if to say, *We did it*, and I'm grinning with pride. An old familiar 80s song plays on the speakers. "Don't You (Forget About Me)" by Simple Minds. Everyone claps and Calder whistles. Toto runs into the aisle and spins around in circles with excitement.

Jesus, I wish I could have shared this moment with my wife.

I'm in a daze through pictures, and it isn't until a new song is playing in the reception hall that I snap out of it. The reception is small, just family, but it feels right. My oldest daughter beams happily at me.

I reach for her and touch a sparkly diamond stud in her ear.

"Something borrowed," she whispers sadly. "Vienna sent them."

Guilt settles in the pit of my belly. I don't regret killing Heath Berkley—not after what he did to Brie and Duvan. I do, however, regret that it put a wedge between Brie and her best friend. Brie confided in me that as much as Vee wanted to come to the wedding, she wouldn't be able to be around me without "accidentally" stabbing me while I wasn't looking. Not to mention, she's still pissed as hell that we "stole" her kill. Apparently she was saving Esteban for a rainy day. Well it rained that day and my wife and I seized the opportunity. Carpe fucking diem.

Another song comes on, dragging me from my dark thoughts.

"Father-daughter dance," she says with a smile as she takes my hand.

I chuckle and bring her hand to my lips before kissing it. "May I have this dance, princess?"

She nods and she reminds me of the little girl from years ago who'd dress up and make me play the prince from her storybooks. I never had the heart to tell her I was the villain. Today, she doesn't look at me any differently. As if I've always been her hero.

"Which song, Daddy?"

Ren stands beside the speakers grinning. "I have just the one for you two."

When Bill Medley's "(I've Had) the Time of My Life" comes on, I choke up. Her brown eyes shimmer with tears as I hug her to me. The song is perfect, and dancing with her is even better.

"Daddy," she whispers. "I'm pregnant again. We just found out."

I snap my stare to hers. "Again?"

She laughs. "Again. Ren promises me we can do this. I'm not so sure. The twins are hard."

"Brie baby, you can do whatever you set your heart to. You've always been strong like your mother. She'd be so fucking proud of you. I know I sure as hell am."

A tear races down her cheek. "Thank you, Daddy."

"Now let's hope this baby looks like you and not like Ren," I tease with a grin.

We both chuckle and the rest of the dance is free of conversation. Just enjoying the moment. I don't ever want to let go, but much too soon, the song ends, and Ren whisks her away to dance. Their eyes are glued to one another, and the love radiating from them is overwhelming. I hope it never wavers for a second. My daughter deserves all the love in the world.

"Daddy," Toto chirps as she tugs on my pant leg. "Dance."

I tug her into my arms and dance much faster to the beat with my baby girl in my arms. She almost falls asleep, until Calder's big mouth takes over the microphone.

"I'd like to dedicate this song to Teev," he says with a shit-eating grin before the *Blue's Clues* theme song starts playing. This perks Toto back up as she starts singing loudly.

"Teev! Teev!" she screeches happily and then squirms out of my arms to go chase after her favorite uncle. Or is it brother-in-law now? Fuck, I really messed up the family tree.

"You're getting soft in your old age," Baylee says. "I think I even saw you crying."

I smirk and regard the angel in the teal dress. "I don't cry," I snap.

She laughs. "Don't try that villainous shit on me. You don't intimidate me anymore."

"You said 'shit' in church," I grumble, but a smile sneaks its way out.

I snag her wrist and she lifts a brow at me.

"Dance?"

My hand gets forcibly removed from hers and War flashes me an annoyed glare. "Nope. This one's mine." He pulls her away to dance closely with her, their sleeping baby sandwiched between them. The sight of them makes me happy. I'm glad that fucker lived after me shooting him in one of my crazed moments. I'm glad he stole my girl from me. So fucking glad.

I scan the room and can't help but think of who we're missing. The girl who I made mine. The girl who rocked my world to its core. The girl who stole my heart and my soul.

My Hannah Bananas.

My goddamned wife.

My everything.

But it's better this way.

Right?

EPILOGUE
Gabe

Five years later...

"TIME TO COME INSIDE," I HOLLER OUT THE back door. "Dinner's ready."

When I walk back to the kitchen to start dishing out the kids' plates, I groan to find Land still swinging despite Toto's obvious attempts to boss him around. Her blonde hair is in uneven pigtails because I kind of suck at doing little girl hair. They bounce each time she yells at him and points at the house. He sticks his tongue out at her but refuses to get off the swing. *Little shit.*

I put their plates in the refrigerator to cool off while I go round up my kids. As soon as I step out onto the back porch, Land flies off the swing set Ren put together for us several years back. He regards me with an innocent stare. Problem is, that little boy is just like his momma. The innocent looks don't work on me. Especially when I know he's been bad.

"In the house, Toto," I tell my daughter.

She huffs. "Daddy, you promised you'd start calling me Toni Lynn. Jackie at school says I'm the dog from *The Wizard of Oz*."

That little Jackie is a fucking bully, and if I knew where she lived, I'd scare the living daylights out of the mini bitch so she'd leave my Toto alone.

"Okay, sweet girl. Go get the plates out of the refrigerator please," I instruct.

She hugs me before running inside. When I turn my attention to Land, he manages to produce tears for theatrics. I hate seeing my kids cry, and this kid fucking knows it.

"Come here."

He runs over to me and hugs my legs. "I'm sorry, Daddy."

I scoop the tiny thing into my arms and kiss his messy dark hair. "Don't rile your sister up, okay?"

He nods and rests his head on my shoulder as we go back inside. Once they've both washed up and are at the table, Toto takes it upon herself to say grace.

"Dear Jesus. Thank you for this yummy food

Daddy made. I love you and Daddy and Mommy and all the squirrels that eat the bird seed out of the feeders. Amen." She beams sweetly at me.

Land huffs. "What about me?"

"What about you?"

"Daddy," Land cries out and glares at his sister. "She said she doesn't love me."

I groan. "Your sister loves you—"

"No I don't," Toto argues.

"Daddy!"

"Toto," I grumble. "Tell your brother you love him."

"No," she says before bursting into tears. "H-He's mean and he doesn't listen. I hate him."

They start yelling at each other, both of them crying now, and I rub my palm across my face. This parenting thing is hard to do alone.

"I miss Mommy," Land wails.

I manage to calm them both down and urge them to eat a little more. They both end up passing out the moment I put a movie on after dinner. I tuck them both into bed and take my time picking up the house. Tomorrow, they'll just ransack it again. If I don't clean every night before bed, it's fucking atrocious by the end of the week. Once the alarm is set, so I'll know if they escape the house, I go to my room and grab my lanyard from the top of my closet and slip it over my head. I make a pass through the kitchen, snagging a few things, before I head down to the basement for some me time. Daddies need me time.

The door is triple locked and tricky to unlock with all the shit in my hands, which is why I put the key on a lanyard, but I eventually get it open. It's quiet, but I'm not alarmed. My footsteps are heavy as I thud down the stairs. When I reach the bottom, my head darts to the left. Always to the left.

God, what a beautiful sight.

"Hey, babe," Hannah chirps, her eyes never leaving the screen in front of her.

"Who's winning?" I ask as I set down her plate of leftovers on the table just outside her door.

"Daddy," she groans.

I smirk to see War wearing the same intense expression as her on the screen. Those two spend countless hours playing chess online together. I'm pretty sure he kicks her ass every time, but it doesn't stop her from trying to win.

"Where are the kids?"

"Asleep. They were both tired as fuck. If I would have brought them down, they'd have begged to spend the night with you and that would have just led to more temper tantrums," I grunt.

I grab on to one of the bars outside her cell and stare in at her. Five years ago, I discovered a way to keep my wife without having her be a danger to herself or others. I didn't have to kill her. And while we were in Buenaventura, Ren did me a solid and finished out this basement for me so I could keep her safe. And everyone else safe *from her*.

My gaze skims over her makeshift prison. There's plenty of space for my girl to roam. She has a comfortable bed that we can both sleep in easily, a bathroom complete with a tub, and a table. Her space is painted in bright colors and the kids' drawings decorate the walls. It looks like any other room in our home—except this room has bars and a locked door. My little inmate has been sentenced for life. And, thank fuck, she's happy.

Getting her inside it proved to be tricky, though, but once she realized I had no intention of killing her, she settled into her new home easily. It gives her peace of mind, knowing she can still have her family but that when the dark thoughts consume her, she can't hurt them.

At one time, I didn't have an answer when it came to Hannah. I thought I would have to kill her. Hell, that's the reason I brought her to Colombia with me. Despite my conversations with Ren about making her a cell, I'd had my doubts it could work. After she and I had eliminated Esteban, I had my hand around her throat. I almost murdered my wife in the pouring rain. It would have been easy to dump her beside Esteban's body. But goddamn was she beautiful. Mine. I was too fucking selfish to let her go. Ren and I would have to make it work. We *did* make it work.

"Checkmate," War says smugly.

I laugh and Hannah shoots me the bird. "Goodnight, Daddy. Same time tomorrow?"

"Of course, sweetheart."

They end the call and she sits up in the bed on her knees. My little hellion is the picture of innocence in her pink T-shirt and jean shorts. But the moment she starts stripping off her shirt, I'm reminded of how not-so-innocent she is.

"You coming in here, babe?" she purrs.

I laugh as I rip off my own T-shirt. "Fuck yeah I am. I've been dealing with bad ass kids all day. I need some mommy and daddy alone time."

She giggles and tugs away her bra, freeing her luscious tits. We both pull off the rest of our clothes pretty much at the same time. Now that my dick is heavy but free, I unlock the door to her cell.

"I'm hungry for you right now," she says, her voice husky. "Dinner can wait."

I chuckle as I saunter in and lock the door behind me. "Didn't I already feed you my cock today while the kids were at school?"

She lies back on the soft bed, her blonde hair spilling on the pillow around her, and bites her lip as she caresses her tits. "You know you have to feed your little animal often."

I growl as I pounce. Her squeals are music to my ears when my mouth finds her neck. I may be old as fuck but this girl keeps me young and on my toes. Never a dull moment with this one. She wraps her long legs around my waist and urges me closer. My fingers tangle in her pretty hair as she grips my cock to guide me inside her. Once I push into her, we both groan in unison.

This is exactly where I'm supposed to be.

"I love you," I breathe against her perfect plump lips. "I love you so goddamned much. All of this is for you." I thrust into her hard enough to make her cry out. "You know this, right? It's always been for you."

She nods and kisses me hard. Our bodies are one as I fuck my wife right into an explosive orgasm. I'll eventually get mine but until then, I plan on pleasuring her with my tongue and fingers.

For most of my life, I screwed shit up and took

the wrong paths. It was engrained in me. But with Hannah, I did something right. With my kids, I did something right. Even the bad guys can be good every once in awhile. I try not to make it a habit. Don't want to get soft, like War.

"Oh, God!" my wife cries out in ecstasy, her body clenching hard around mine.

"That's it, sweet girl. Give it all to me. It's mine," I growl. "*You're* mine."

She unravels with my name on her lips, and it makes me so goddamned happy. This life—our life— is perfect. Undeserving but ours. Nobody will ever take this away from us. Not now. Not ever.

Happy endings aren't for villains…

But we fucking take them anyway.

This really *is* **THE END**, baby.

Dear Reader,

Thank you for going on this epic and twisted journey with me! Your support has been amazing! I ask that you PLEASE don't spoil the plot or ending of this book in your reviews. I want everyone to be just as surprised as you. The twists and turns are designed for your enjoyment. They aren't as fun when you know what they are going in. Thank you so much for helping me with this!

Sincerely,
K Webster

Ward (Alma Negra Mexican Mafia, 1)

Vienna Gomez

"He's vicious, mi diablita," Diego grumbles, irritation seeping into his tone as he leans back in the leather chair that used to belong to my father. "Go sit your skinny ass back in the car where it's safe."

I gape at him with a snarled lip. "Skinny? Have you *looked* at me lately?"

His lazy stare skims over my body, as I'm perched on the edge of the desk, lingering at my larger-than-normal breasts. "You got fat tits. That's hot." Then his light brown eyes dart to mine. "Of course you'd take issue with *that* word. Skinny. Vicious, however, doesn't even make you flinch. You have a fetish for villains. Shall I murder him as soon as he walks in?" A possessive growl rumbles from him. "I'm the only villain you're allowed to want."

I toss him a wicked grin. "You're my favorite villain," I say. "And don't kill this baddie. We need him. He's promised to buy a shit-ton of coke from us."

"While this is true, it isn't necessary for my

pregnant wife to be a part of this deal." His nostrils flare and he absently pats at his jacket pocket. When he finds the foil package of gum instead of his cigar, he curses. "The fucking things I do for you, woman."

I beam at him. When he read smoking around a pregnant woman was bad for the baby during my first pregnancy, he quit lighting up around me. Now that we're halfway along with this pregnancy, he's vowed to do the same. He still bears the same pissed-off glare whenever he finds gum in place of his beloved cigars, though.

I slide my heeled foot along his thigh. "You love me," I tell him. The pointy part of my stiletto pokes at his beautiful cock through his slacks. Wakes that boy right up.

He grabs my ankle almost painfully. "More than fucking anything."

"And you love our son."

His eyes light up at the mention of a son. We don't know for sure, but Tatiana says the heartbeat belongs to a boy, or so she thinks. My gut tells me it's another girl but I don't dare torture my poor husband any more on that sore subject.

Reaching forward, he grabs my hips and pulls me into his lap, so that I straddle him. His large palms roam over my ass. When he buries his nose in my cleavage, which is exposed in the low-cut black dress, I clutch his hair and tilt my head back. Hot breath tickles me as he sucks and nibbles the flesh. Being pregnant, my hormones are out of control. I can't seem to get enough of him. At least several times a day, I'm all over him begging for sex.

Well, I don't have to beg too hard.

"Fuck me, mi motherfucker," I demand, my fingers desperately tugging at his tie.

His teeth sink into my breast, causing me to cry out. I'm three seconds from pulling his cock out of his slacks when someone clears their throat from behind me.

Diego and I both jolt in surprise. He lifts me quickly before depositing me on the desk. Then, he stands and regards our guest. I take Diego's place in his chair so I no longer have my back to them.

"Señor Celestino," Jorge says in introduction before he steps outside the office, closing the door behind him.

I drag my gaze to our visitor. Our future business partner. The first thing I notice is he's a giant. Tall. Like freakishly tall. And, my God, is he stacked. His muscles are bulging so much that it's as if his expensive suit is painted on him.

"Diego Gomez," my husband greets in a cool,

calm tone. All playfulness from earlier is gone. "Pleased to meet you Señor Celestino."

The man's surly gesture makes him appear stand-offish. "Call me Tomás," he says, a low rumble in his throat. Diego growls all the time. Possessive and sexy. Tomás's growl, however, is feral and kind of scary. I shiver and pull open the side drawer where Diego's Glock sits. I feel safer when I can see it.

"Tomás," Diego says, his voice warming. "I see that you're interested in buying eighty percent of our US export? Eso es una gran cantidad de cocaína, mi amigo."

He's curious about why Tomás wants to buy so much. My Spanish is getting better, although most of what I've learned are the naughty words Diego whispers to me when he's seducing me.

Tomás grunts and crosses his arms over his massive chest. His gaze travels to the window. Black ink from a tattoo crawls up the side of his neck toward his ear. Could be feathers or fire, I can't be sure. He snaps his head back toward us and locks eyes with me.

Dark, almost black, soulless eyes.

Alma Negra.

Mexian mafia.

Diego gave me the run down on this Tomás

Celestino guy. The Celestinos—four dangerous brothers—are the leaders of one of the most vicious West Coast organized crime groups. According to Diego, they're not refined like the Italians—they sure as hell dress like them though—or brilliant masterminds like the Russians.

This mafia is ruthless.

Brutal.

Rich thugs.

Killers through and through.

But they survive like cockroaches. They infest and overpower everything they want to be involved in. Sex trafficking. Drugs. Prison control. Government corruption.

They are powerful and loaded.

Perfect customers for us to do business with.

"I knew Heath," Tomás bites out, his tone icy.

I tense and pin him with a fiery glare. "Super."

One corner of his lips twitch but then his gaze is back on Diego. "You know my offer. The terms are fair, Gomez. I didn't drive all the way from LA to San Diego to negotiate. I came here to make a fucking deal."

"And what insurance do we have that you don't fuck us over?" Diego asks, leaning his sexy hip against the desk. His butt is bitable in his charcoal grey slacks. I think he wears this particular pair of pants to fuck with my hormones.

"If I wanted to fuck you over," Tomás snarls, "your mujer would be bent over this desk letting me put babies inside her while you watched."

Diego doesn't stiffen or grumble or do anything to indicate he's intimidated by Tomás. Meanwhile, I can't help the shiver of fear that ripples through me. When Diego laughs, loud and boisterous, I relax. He looks back at me and winks. "Daddy Diego likes a ballsy asshole. Don't I, mi diablita?"

I snort because he's referring to me. "You do, mi motherfucker."

Tomás stares at me and his eyebrow twitches slightly. Almost as if the terrifying prick finds us amusing. But something tells me it takes a lot to make this dude smile. I don't have the patience nor the time for that.

"You fuck us over, you die," I bite out as I reach past the Glock for a package of Skittles. I rip it open and pop a green one in my mouth before pinning him with a hard glare. "You fuck us over, we kill every single one of your brothers. Even the youngest one. The one with the gentle eyes and the soft smile. What's his name?" I taunt, chomping on my juicy candy. "Oh, that's right. Zacarías. I think he's about my age. We'd probably be fast friends, ol' Zac and I. I bet he falls for girls easily. Especially pretty ones. Heart on his sleeve type of guy—"

"Enough!" Tomás roars, his chest heaving. His fists are at his sides, and I swear he's seconds from attacking me.

Nerve. Struck.

I beam at him. "Now that I've made my point, I trust you won't fuck with us." I pull a yellow Skittle out of the bag and roll it across the desk toward Diego. I fucking hate the yellow ones.

He picks it up and tosses it in his mouth. "Since we have the pleasantries out of the way, I suppose we can move forward and do business."

Tomás's nostrils flare as he glares at me.

Diego laughs and struts over to our new client. He slaps a hand on the man's shoulder. "Don't worry, hermano, she scares the fuck out of me too."

I shrug and eat another beloved green candy. "Nobody fucks with the queen."

Tomás tears his furious stare from me to regard Diego. "Keep your queen of the fucking crazy ass cartel in Colombia, and we have ourselves a deal."

Diego laughs again. God, I love the sound of his boyish laugh. Warms every part of me from the inside out. "You and I both know, Señor Celestino," he says as he offers Tomás a hand. "Mi diablita does whatever the fuck she wants. But I *will* sell you la cocaína. And you *will* keep your word."

Tomás grunts but firmly shakes his hand. Everything in the man's empty black eyes says he's not one to go back on his word. These delicious Hispanic men and their integrity…they don't break their promises.

But Momma Gomez likes insurance.

I reach into the drawer and reluctantly trade my Skittles for my knife. Tomás's eyes are on my every move. If he wanted to kill me, he could. Men like him are catastrophic. Forces of fucking nature. Men like him don't move out of fear because they don't see me as a threat.

They haven't met Queen V.

"Nothing says '*I do*' like a little blood contract," I tell him sweetly as I stand and walk over to him. "Give me your arm."

His jaw clenches but he remains motionless. After the longest stare down, he shrugs out of his black blazer and begins unbuttoning his shirt at the wrist. Once he rolls up the sleeve to reveal a veiny tattooed forearm, he offers me his arm.

"Good boy." I grin at him before grabbing his wrist. Carefully, I carve the letters: D. V. G. Blood runs from the slices and drips onto the concrete office floor.

The murderous glare he gives me is scary as hell, but I ignore it.

"Nice doing business with you, Mr. Celestino," I chirp before sitting back down at the desk.

His nostrils flare and he gives a slight shake of his head. "You're a crazy bitch, you know that?"

"Of course *I* already know this. It's *you* who's just finding out." I pluck the Skittles bag out and start fishing for another green one. "And it'll do you good to remember that too."

He narrows his creepy-as-fuck eyes at me and cracks his neck. Disregarding the blood, he fastens the button of his shirt and then slides his suit jacket back on. I'm awarded one more of his threatening glares before he stalks out of the office without another word.

"Such a bad girl," Diego chides, flashing me a wicked grin.

I smile at him while rubbing my swollen belly. "I'm a villain. It's what I do."

Tomás Celestino* and the *Alma Negra Mexican Mafia* series are coming soon!

PLAYLIST

Listen on Spotify

"The Way" by Saigon Kick

"Love is on the Way" by Saigon Kick

"The Way I Do" by Bishop Briggs

"Everything In Its Right Place" by Radiohead

"The Red" by Chevelle

"Heathens" by Twenty One Pilots

"Mad World (feat. Gary Jules)" by Michael Andres

"Never Tear Us Apart" by INXS

"Take Me To Church" by Hozier

"This is War" by Thirty Seconds to Mars

"Monster" by Meg Myers

"Stubborn Love" by The Lumineers

"To Be Alone" by Hozier

"Heart Heart Head" by Meg Myers

"The Funeral" by Band of Horses

"Desire" by Meg Myers

"Where Is My Mind?" by Pixies

"Love is Strange" by Mickey & Slyvia

"Stand By Me" by Ki:Theory

"The Sound of Silence" by Simon & Garfunkel

"Sweet Dreams" by Marilyn Manson

"Even Though Our Love Is Doomed" by Garbage

"Fade Into You" by Mazzy Star

"Last Goodbye" by Jeff Buckley

"Black" by Pearl Jam

"Madness" by Muse

"Wild Horses" by Bishop Briggs

"Are You Alone Now?" by Dead Sea Empire

"Sick & Wrong" by The Mayfield Four

"High" by Sir Sly

"Sucker For Pain" by Lil Wayne

"Mad Love" by Bush

Books by K Webster

The Breaking the Rules Series:

Broken (Book 1)

Wrong (Book 2)

Scarred (Book 3)

Mistake (Book 4)

Crushed (Book 5 – a novella)

The Vegas Aces Series:

Rock Country (Book 1)

Rock Heart (Book 2)

Rock Bottom (Book 3)

The Becoming Her Series:

Becoming Lady Thomas (Book 1)

Becoming Countess Dumont (Book 2)

Becoming Mrs. Benedict (Book 3)

War & Peace Series:

This is War, Baby (Book 1)

This is Love, Baby (Book 2)

This Isn't Over, Baby (Book 3)

This Isn't You, Baby (Book 4)

This is Me, Baby (Book 5)

This Isn't Fair, Baby (Book 6)

This is the End, Baby (Book 7 – a novella)

2 Lovers Series:

Text 2 Lovers (Book 1)

Hate 2 Lovers (Book 2)

Alpha & Omega Duet:

Alpha & Omega (Book 1)

Omega & Love (Book 2)

Pretty Stolen Dolls Duet:

Pretty Stolen Dolls (Book 1)

Pretty Lost Dolls (Book 2)

Taboo Treats:

Bad Bad Bad

Standalone Novels:

Apartment 2B

Love and Law

Moth to a Flame

Erased

The Road Back to Us

Surviving Harley

Give Me Yesterday

Running Free

Dirty Ugly Toy

Zeke's Eden

Sweet Jayne

Untimely You

Mad Sea

Whispers and the Roars

Schooled by a Senior

B-Sides and Rarities

Blue Hill Blood by Elizabeth Gray

ACKNOWLEDGEMENTS

Thank you to my husband…you always have my back and I love you so much!

A huge thank you to my Krazy for K Webster's Books reader group. You all are insanely supportive and I can't thank you enough. I'm so thankful for the support of this series and my books overall. You ladies rock!

A big thanks to my favorite villainous bad boy character, Gabe Sharpe. You started this book with a bang, made us hate you through a lot of the series, forced us to feel compassion and love for you, and ultimately you ended the series on a note that I'm proud of. You'll always be my favorite.

A gigantic thank you to my betas who read this story. Elizabeth Clinton, Ella Stewart, Shannon Miller, Amy Bosica, Brooklyn Miller, Robin Martin, Amy Simms, Jessica Viteri, Amanda Söderlund, and Jessica Hollyfield, you all helped make this story even better. Your feedback and early reading is important to this entire process and I can't thank you enough.

Also, a big thank you to Vanessa Renee Place for proofreading this story!! Love you!

A big thank you to my author friends who have given me your friendship and your support. You have no idea how much that means to me.

Thank you to all of my blogger friends both big and small that go above and beyond to always share my stuff. You all rock! #AllBlogsMatter

I am totally thankful for my author group, the COPA gals, for being there when I need to take a load off and whine. Y'all rock!

Vanessa with Prema Editing, thanks so much for editing this book! You rock! Your love for this series is important to the finished product! Also a huge thank you to Jessica Descent for being second set of eyes!

Thank you Stacey Blake for being a super star as always when formatting my books and in general. I love you! I love you! I love you!

A big thanks to my PR gal, Nicole Blanchard. You are

fabulous at what you do and keep me on track!

Lastly but certainly not least of all, thank you to all of the wonderful readers out there that are willing to hear my story and enjoy my characters like I do. It means the world to me!

ABOUT THE AUTHOR

K Webster is the author of dozens of romance books in many different genres including contemporary romance, historical romance, paranormal romance, dark romance, romantic suspense, and erotic romance. When not spending time with her hilarious and handsome husband and two adorable children, she's active on social media connecting with her readers.

Her other passions besides writing include reading and graphic design. K can always be found in front of her computer chasing her next idea and taking action. She looks forward to the day when she will see one of her titles on the big screen.

Join K Webster's newsletter to receive a couple of updates a month on new releases and exclusive content. To join, all you need to do is go to http://authorkwebster.us10.list-manage.com/ subscribe?u=36473e274a1bf9597b508ea72&id=96366b-b08e).

Facebook: www.facebook.com/authorkwebster

Blog: authorkwebster.wordpress.com/

Twitter:twitter.com/KristiWebster

Email: kristi@authorkwebster.com

Goodreads:
www.goodreads.com/user/show/10439773-k-webster

Instagram: instagram.com/kristiwebster

A sneak peek of *Sweet Jayne* (now available)

Prologue

Nadia

I FUCKING HATE DONOVAN JAYNE.

A furious scream is lodged in my throat, but one desperate, pleading look from my mother, and I'm trotting away from the asshole in our expensive kitchen toward the front door with my lips firmly pressed together.

Words like, *Fuck you,* or *Eat shit and die,* or *Stop checking out your seventeen-year-old stepdaughter, you prick,* all remain unsaid and poised on the tip of my tongue that craves to lash out at him. If it weren't for my mother actually loving the asshole, I'd have already given him a piece of my mind.

But she does love him—or so she says. And Mamá deserves any morsel of happiness she can get. She's been unhappy for so long. Ever since Papá died in an accident at the mill he worked at, just outside of Buenos Aires six years ago, she's been lost. The pretty smile that used to light up her face had darkened. It was by chance that she ran into the cocky hotel and resort magnate, Donovan Jayne. She'd been working as a housekeeper at one of the biggest hotels in Argentina. During her rounds, she pushed through his door, ready to collect the dirty towels thinking no one was in at the time. He was just coming out of the bathroom after a shower as she was entering. She apologized profusely and went to leave, but he wouldn't let her go. Love at first sight, they both claim.

Gag.

How anyone could love that self-centered asshole is beyond me. He not only uprooted us and moved us to Colorado to marry her, but I also had to leave all of my friends behind during my last year of high school. We'd gone from our simple two-bedroom apartment which Mamá was able to afford in the city on her meager housekeeping salary to a breathtaking mansion on a fucking mountain. But, her smile is back again. Mamá smiles like she did when Papá was still alive and that's the only reason I put up with Donovan's shit.

And by shit, I mean his possessiveness over his "family." The way he struts around this town showing us off like we're a couple of prized horses. But when someone so much as looks at us remotely wrong, he turns into a narcissistic idiot who reminds them who owns this town. *We do*, he says. Quite frankly, I'm embarrassed to be a part of the "we."

Ten more months. I can suck it up, bite my tongue, and let him pull my strings for ten more months. And then I'm off to college. I'm not sure where I'll go yet but it will most definitely be far, far away from Donovan and his superiority complex.

"Nadia Jayne!"

I cringe on the bottom step of the front porch and consider running the rest of the way to the bus stop to avoid having to talk to him. But Donovan doesn't give up so easily. He's shrewd and determined. It's best to let him spout his bullshit and then move on. So, instead, I lift my chin and turn to regard him with a raised eyebrow, no doubt revealing my disdain for him.

"What?" I hiss out my question, hoping the venom in my voice stings.

A small flinch at my tone is the only indication I've hurt him before he quickly masks it away with a look of indifference. He must've gotten ready for work early this morning, as he's already donning a pristine dark grey suit. I've never, not once, seen him *not* in a suit. For thirty-six, he's well-built and handsome. His dark hair is styled in a way that's meant to look messy and his grey-blue eyes are piercing. Always calculating and determining his next move. I'm not blind to the fact that his physical traits are attractive. But it's what's on the inside that makes him a creep. And he's the biggest damn creep around. I've seen the way he looks at me as if he wants to fuck me.

His eyes linger on my bare legs, unhidden by my ridiculously short school uniform because I've purposefully rolled it up as not to appear to look like an old maid on my first day, before he drags them up to meet my simmering gaze. "You forgot your lunch money," he says, waving a crisp hundred-dollar bill at me, "and you forgot to give your old man a hug goodbye."

Anger causes my chest to heat up. I can feel it clawing up my neck, revealing itself to him. His smirk tells me he knows he's struck a chord with me. I fist my hands at my sides to keep from doing something stupid like flipping him off. I'm already grounded from the car he bought me after we officially moved here this summer. I hadn't even gotten to drive it once. *"You talk back around here and your privileges get taken away. My house, my rules."* Fuck him and his house rules.

"You're not my dad," I snap. Visions of my own loving father flit through my head and I feel the familiar ache in my chest at losing him.

He takes a few steps toward me and flashes me a wide grin, revealing perfect, white teeth. "Technically I *am* your daddy. If you forgot, maybe you should check your ID again."

Tears well in my eyes but I clench my jaw. I won't let them spill over and give him the satisfaction of knowing that he can so easily rile me up. But he's right. Donovan's good at what he does. He swoops in, buys property—in this case, my mother and me— and stamps his name all over it. The asshole made sure he legally adopted me so I would bear the Jayne name too.

I'm no longer Nadia Blanco.

As of two months ago, I'm officially Nadia Jayne.

With a huff, I stomp up the steps and make my way up to where he's standing. His eyes glimmer with excitement as I approach. Five bucks says he's sporting a hard-on, too. More heat floods through me, this time making its way to my cheeks, and I shiver at that idea. God, my poor mother.

He holds out the money but when I reach for it, he clutches onto my wrist. His gaze darkens and he affixes me with a firm glare. "Don't embarrass me. The principal at your school sits on the board of my company. I won't have you tarnishing the Jayne name," he says coolly. "I wouldn't want to have to spank you over my knee for being a bad girl."

My jaw drops and I gape at him. I knew the bastard was a pervert but he's crossed over onto a whole new plane of twistedness.

"Oh, don't act so shocked, Nadia. You know I'm not opposed to disciplining you. If I remember correctly, you're still grounded from your car because of your attitude. I'd be more than happy to try other methods of punishment. Clearly, your attitude still fucking sucks. Maybe a little ass whipping will be good for you."

When I try to wriggle my hand out of his grasp, he grips it tighter and pulls me closer. His cologne invades my lungs and I nearly choke from the potent smell.

"¡Te odio!" I hiss. *I hate you.* Jerking my hand away, I take several steps back.

The corner of his mouth lifts up in a devilishly

handsome grin. "Tell me you'll be a good girl."

I glare at him and nod my head, not giving him the satisfaction of my words. His eyes lazily skim over my face and stop at my lips.

"Good," he says, his smile faltering and his eyes finding mine again. "Have a great first day of school, sunshine." His gaze softens for a brief moment. For one tiny second I think Donovan Jayne may even be human. Not some asshole I've been forced to obey until the day I turn eighteen and can bolt. "Come here." His voice is hoarse this time.

With his arrogance taking a surprising backseat for once, I find myself going to him willingly. Almost seeking his comfort for some odd reason. When I'm close enough, he eats up the rest of the distance with his long legs and then his powerful arms are around me, pulling me against his solid chest. The stiffness I always carry when I'm around him melts away as he hugs me. Our hug is different this time. It's not forced for once. His scent, like always, cloaks me and I know from experience I'll smell him all day long. A constant reminder of his iron grip on my life. Today, though, I'm hoping it will give me even an ounce of his confidence as I attempt to make new friends in my new school.

"The boys are all beneath you here," he says with

a playful growl. "I know this because I grew up here. Stay away from them. They don't deserve you."

A small smile tugs at my lips. That's probably the sweetest thing he's ever said to me. I lift my head up and look into his eyes that sparkle with an emotion I can never quite put my finger on. "Maybe I'm not into boys." I quirk up an eyebrow in a challenging way.

His soft features pinch into a hard scowl, momentarily stunning me. "You shouldn't be into anyone. School should be your primary focus. I'll forbid you from dating—boys or girls—if your grades start to suffer."

God, I hate him. How could I have so easily forgotten?

Before releasing me, he pats my ass with one hand and kisses the top of my head. As soon as he pulls away, I snatch the money from his hold and storm away from him. It isn't until I'm halfway down the long gravel driveway that I realize tears are streaking down my cheeks.

"Nadia," he calls out to me, a hint of remorse in his voice.

Swiping away a tear, I turn to regard him. His face has an apology written all over it but his stubborn mouth refuses to let it out.

"What?" I prod.

He scrubs at his cheeks with his palms, an almost angry scowl forming after. His steps are rushed as he strides back over to the front door and swings it open, calling out to me over his shoulder. "Have a good day at school."

I don't respond as the door slams behind him but instead wave him off. If it weren't for him and his "undying" bullshit love for my mother, I'd be texting with my friend Julienne as we speak, trying to figure out a way to skip out on our last class of the day. Instead, I'm in another country, going to a brand new school, and completely friendless with nobody to talk to aside from my mother and annoyingly good-looking stepfather. *Thanks, Daddy.*

Once I reach the road beside the mailbox, I sit down in the grass and ignore the cold morning dew soaking my bottom through my skirt. I swipe the tears away with the back of my hand and try to overlook the fact that my stepfather is a prick. It was stupid to think there was an actual likable person behind the suit and hard eyes. Doubt I'll ever make the mistake of letting my guard down again.

"Please don't tell me you live *there*," a voice calls out from the road.

I look up to the sound of the young voice and see

a girl who looks to be around my age walking toward me. Her hair is dyed black on top and pale blonde underneath. She's got it pulled up in a messy bun that reveals multiple piercings in her ears. The school uniform she's wearing looks just like mine, but wrinkly and slightly baggy.

"Please tell me you're here to help me run away," I joke back.

Her eyebrows furrow together as she approaches and inspects me. "Why are you crying?"

I drop my gaze to my lap and tug at a loose thread on my skirt. "I hate my stepdad."

She plops down beside me and mimics my cross-legged position. I watch with fascination as she pulls out a pack of cigarettes and lights one. "Funny. I hate my stepdad, too."

A puff of smoke surrounds us as she exhales. We sit in silence for a moment while she smokes and I plan ways to kill Donovan.

Finally, she says, "I'm Kasey."

She hands me her cigarette and I gingerly take it from her. I'm not a smoker but I don't want to scare away my first potential friend with being snooty.

"Nadia."

I take a puff and then cough before handing her back the cigarette.

"You new to Aspen High?" she questions.

Glancing up at her, I take in her features. Despite the dark eyeliner and heavy purple lipstick, a pretty face hides beneath. Her hazel eyes look sad, as if she has a whole lifetime of stories to tell.

"Yep. I moved here from Argentina this summer."

Her eyebrows furrow together in confusion. "You don't sound foreign."

I laugh and roll my eyes. "What exactly does foreign sound like?"

Her cheeks turn slightly pink but she tries to hide her embarrassment with another puff of her cigarette. "I don't know. Like, you don't speak another language or have an accent or whatever."

"Los Americanos pueden ser tan ignorantes," I tell her with a smile. *Americans can be so ignorant.* "Is that better?"

She scrunches her nose up at me. "What did you say?"

"I insulted you," I say shrugging my shoulders. "It takes out all the fun if I tell you."

"Bitch," she says with a grin and flips me off.

I run my fingers through my long, dark locks that are still smooth from straightening them this morning. "In my old school, we had to learn both English and Spanish. Everyone there could speak both languages fluently. My mother always drilled into me that knowing multiple languages would help me be successful one day, especially if I went to college in another country like the U.S. Her dream, not mine. I guess her dream came true."

She laughs. "College. Must be nice to have that option."

"Everyone has that option," I say with a frown, furrowing my brows together.

She stands quickly and flicks the half-smoked cigarette into the street. "Not when you're trailer trash," she says and points at a mobile home through the tree line across the road. "When you're poor, your only option is to find a job in this shitty-ass town and pop out a couple of babies. Your destiny, when you're like me, is being some asshole's punching bag. A wife to a drunk who beats you. You have no future. No love. Happily fucking ever after. Just ask my mom."

I lift my chin to see her visibly shaking. Not really knowing anything about this girl and also not wanting to upset her, I rush to blurt out the first thing that comes to mind. "Cheers," I say with a sneer, "to moms everywhere who married fucking assholes."

She snaps her gaze to mine and a small smile plays at her lips. With a few rapid blinks, she chases away the despondency in her eyes and is once again composed. "Cheers."

"You know," I tell her as I pick a blade of wet grass and try to tie it in a knot, "you could go to college. You don't have to be like your mom."

A sardonic chuckle is tossed back at me. "God, you sound like Taylor," she says wistfully but then her bottom lip trembles.

"Who's Taylor?" I question, wondering about her sudden mood change.

She gapes at me as if I've lost my mind but then waves off the question. "He's just someone I used to know." I sense the lie in her words. He was more than that. Much more than that. "Besides," she says, changing the subject, "what money would I go to college with, anyway?"

This time it's me who looks at her like she just crawled out from under a rock. "Um, grants? Scholarships? Duh."

She shrugs her shoulders. "Maybe. But college isn't what I want to do."

I wait for her to elaborate but she doesn't. Finally, after a few minutes, I ask. "Well, what do you want to do then?"

She turns to regard me with a look of embarrassment, her teeth tugging at her bottom lip. The expression makes her seem younger, a stark contrast to her harsh makeup. Kasey hides behind the emo look for some reason. I wonder what she'd look like with her natural hair color, whatever that may be.

"You'll just laugh at me."

I roll my eyes. "Fine, I'll go first. Mine is laughable too. We can laugh together."

The corners of her lips draw up into a small smile. "Okay then."

"I always wanted to be a cook. Maybe a sous chef or a pastry chef. I'm not one hundred percent sure, but I love food. Clearly," I mutter and motion at my curvy body.

She places her hands on her hips and arches a brow at me. "Are you kidding me right now? I'd kill to have your body. I'm still waiting for the boob fairy to show up and sprinkle me with some titty dust. But obviously she accidentally spilled the whole jar on you."

We both burst out into a fit of giggles and I swipe at tears—this time from laughter.

"Be careful what you wish for," I tease. "Now tell me already."

She lights up another cigarette as if she's working up the courage to start talking. After a couple of drags, she meets my gaze. "I want to work at a day care."

"That seems completely doable. Is this like a gothic day care?" I question with a grin. "Would all the babies wear Metallica T-shirts and cuss? Would they take smoke breaks instead of recess?"

"Bite me." She laughs and kicks some rocks from my driveway toward me.

I'm still smiling when a squeal of tires draws my attention down the road. Kasey flicks her still burning cigarette into the street and we both watch as a black SUV comes barreling down the street, headed our way.

"Slow down, asshole!" she yells and flips off the vehicle as it nears.

A screeching of the tires deafens me as it comes to a complete stop right in front of where I'm sitting beside the mailbox. The door is wrenched open, and I see black combat boots first before seeing who they belong to.

Flickering my gaze over to Kasey, I notice the nervousness on her face as she starts to take a step back. When I jerk my head back over to the car, I see why.

A big man, dressed entirely in black with a ski mask covering his face, is charging for her. It happens so quickly that I'm frozen with my ass planted on the earth and I can only watch what's unfolding right in front of me. She lets out an ear-piercing screech as he runs for her. Kasey doesn't make it far before he's got his massive arms wrapped around her middle. Her long legs kick wildly around her as he drags her back toward the car. The moment her terrified gaze meets mine, I jolt into action.

"No! Stop!" I scream as I scramble to my knees when he passes by me. "Let her go."

He grunts in exertion at her struggling but has the ability to meet my stare. The eyes behind the mask are wild and crazed. I'm trying to get a better look at the man when he raises his knee in the air. The bottom of his gigantic boot slams into my cheek with the force of a hurricane. Blackness explodes in front of me, blinding me from the man who is forcefully kidnapping my friend, and I fall back into the grass, slamming my head against the ground.

As I try to regain my wits, I hear a car door slam once as he shoves her into the vehicle. Another slam sounds after he climbs back in. The SUV screeches into drive and hauls ass down the road. A wave of dizziness washes over me but I quickly roll to my side to try and read the license plate.

Too blurry.

Too far away.

Another blanket of darkness clouds my vision

and I black out.

I'm not sure if it's minutes or hours later when I hear Donovan's concerned voice and I slowly regain consciousness.

"Nadia, baby," he murmurs as he cradles my head in his hand. "What happened?"

My eyes are fixated on the road where Kasey's half-smoked cigarette rolls around in the wind, the cherry still red on the end. When I don't respond, he slides his arms beneath me and pulls me into them against his chest. Normally, I hate Donovan but right now, I need him.

I need him to hold me like Papá would have.

To tell me everything's going to be okay.

For him to assure me that Kasey and the man who took her were all just a silly figment of my teenage imagination.

"Selene!" Donovan hollers to Mamá. "Call 911! I think Nadia was assaulted. Her nose is bleeding and she's disoriented."

His dark eyebrows are pinched together in genuine concern and it comforts me.

"Kasey," I murmur and blink slowly. A massive migraine is wrapping its evil claws around my skull and crushing in on me. "He took Kasey."

His eyes widen and he darts his gaze back down the street as if to see the vehicle that's now long gone. When he turns to look back down at me, he presses a chaste kiss to my forehead and then pins me with a searing stare. "Shhh. We'll tell the police. But you're safe now, Nadia. I'll make sure nothing happens to you." He then curses, "Jesus Christ, it could have been you instead."

I want to feel comforted that it wasn't me but I don't. All I can think about is her terrified expression. The fact that someone took her. How, if the police aren't able to find her and soon, she'll never get to hold the babies at the day care like she dreamed about.

Someone could abuse her. Rape her even.

And what's worse, they may kill her.

Kasey was right.

She has no future.

Donovan carries me up the steps of our house where moments earlier he was acting like a pervert and fondling my ass. It seems so miniscule in comparison to what Kasey is now facing—being taken by some twisted predator. While I was annoyed and creeped out over my stepdad, she's probably scared out of her fucking mind in the clutches of a lunatic. I really am just a spoiled brat. A girl who doesn't know how good she really has it.

"Please help me find her," I beg him with tears in my eyes.

He stares at me for a long minute, a frown tarnishing his otherwise handsome face. When he eventually snaps out of whatever thought held him, he nods. "I'll do what I can, baby. I swear to fucking God, I will do everything in my power to find her." The intensity in his vow to find a random girl who is a stranger to him shocks me. A newfound respect for him begins taking root deep inside me.

In this moment, I realize Donovan might not be so bad. The glimmer of the man he'd shown me earlier is making a reappearance. I see the promise in his penetrating gaze—a promise to make me happy. To indulge his little girl.

And if sucking up to Donovan is what it takes to find Kasey, then that's what I'll do.

I have to save her.

I swear to God, I'll find and save her somehow.

She'll have her future.

Her happy ending.

I'll make sure of it.

One

Kasper

Nearly ten years later...

ATE.

A four letter word that has consumed nine years of my life.

Nine fucking years.

It's dictated my every thought, my every action, and my every move. I've faded into a ghost of the person I was before and gladly taken on a new image. A new persona.

I've become a nightmare.

Sure, you could call me one of the good guys. But I know better. Despite my career choices and the way

I carry myself for all to see, I'm something dark and bitter beneath the surface. Beneath the lopsided grins and cocky exterior, I'm a hell storm of fury and rage.

My fire burns for one person.

So bright and brilliant—exceedingly hot.

I crave to decimate everything in her path, including her.

I've made it my life's mission to destroy hers. I don't want to kill her. Nah, that'd be too fucking easy for the bitch. Instead, I want to take every single thing she cares about and ruin it. I want her to watch as I rip and tear her entire life to shreds, only to then stomp what's left into the dirt.

She needs to pay for being a stupid, useless cunt.

"You still coming by on Saturday for the game?" Rhodes questions from the doorway of my office. "Ashley was pissed she made pigs in a blanket just for you, only for you to not show up last weekend. You know how emotional her pregnant ass gets, Ghost."

I smirk at him and shrug my shoulders. Jason Rhodes and I go way back. All the way to our high school years. He's one of the few guys at the station I actually like and don't mind hanging out with. "I don't know, man. You know how it gets this time of year. Everyone wants shit built so they can enjoy it for spring. I've already done two decks and a gazebo and we're only two weeks into November. If I'm free, I'll stop by."

He shakes his head. "You work too much. What, being lieutenant and Chief's bitch isn't enough? You just have to spend all your free time building shit too?" His radio beeps and he responds that he's en route. Before he turns to leave, he flashes me a mischievous grin. "Ash said Cassidy will be there. She's been wanting to get back on your cold dick since you porked her at my thirtieth birthday party last month."

"Blow me, Detective," I grunt, grabbing my dick. "Don't you have better shit to do than worry about my sex life?"

He chuckles and saunters down the hallway leading away from my office and calls over his shoulder, "Just think about it. Blow-jobs, lil' smokies, and a lot of beer. What better way to spend a Saturday night?"

When he's gone, the smile falls from my lips and I flip the file closed I'd been working on. I pinch the bridge of my nose and close my eyes. Just like always, my mind flits to her.

The bitch.

The one responsible for my sister.

Gut-churning hatred filled my insides.

With a huff, I open my eyes and start slamming

files into my drawers. My shift ended a half hour ago and I'm tired as hell. I just want to go home, do a little research, and pass the fuck out.

Once my desk is cleared, I pull my drawer key from my pocket and open it. Inside is one single file. A file that I've obsessed over ever since I joined the Aspen Police Department five years ago. At the time, I thought it held answers to the questions that plagued me. I assumed I'd unravel the mysteries nobody else had been able to.

Instead, I found *her* statement.

I found *her* pictures.

I found *her* high-dollar lawyer's business card and *her* stepfather's information. Fucking Donovan Jayne of all people.

But nowhere did I find any clues about the prick who took Kasey. The stupid bitch simply watched while some sick fuck stole my sister and did nothing. Absolutely nothing. She watched as he—*the man who was dressed all in black wearing a mask*—shoved Kasey into his black SUV—*no make or model*—and drove away.

"I don't remember."

"I don't know."

Those two phrases were used more times than I could count in her report. But that's a lie because I did count. In fact, I highlighted every single time she *didn't remember*. All twenty-six times. And all eighteen times she *didn't know*.

The rich bitch went on to have a fucking fabulous life.

Meanwhile, my little sister was probably dismembered and at the bottom of some fucking lake right now.

With a roar, I slam my fist on my desk, causing my cold cup of coffee to slosh and splatter onto the file. I flip to the back and run my fingers over the last date recorded. The last time I had eyes on the dumb bitch. She'd gone to college for a few years in LA. Then, she'd come back to Colorado to work at the Aspen Pines Lodge at the top of the mountain with Donovan. I thought it would be my chance. That I could finally seize the opportunity to make her life a living hell. I'd even put plans in motion to make that happen.

But then she fucking vanished.

For three goddamned years.

And I've been trying to locate her ever since.

My phone buzzes and I see a text from my mother which causes the stale coffee in my stomach to sour.

Mom: I miss you. Come see us at The Joint.

Rolling my eyes, I ignore her text and shove the file back into my desk. Once it's locked up, I shoot her a reply.

Me: Maybe. Is asshole there?

I stand from my desk and stretch before swiping my keys from the corner. I'm not in the mood to see Dale today but I know Mom will just harass the fuck out of me until I come visit, so I decide to drop by for a few minutes to get it out of the way, on my way home from work. Before I leave my office, I do a cursory sweep to make sure nothing is out of place. Rhodes makes fun of me, says I'm a sociopath or some shit, but I pay him no attention. It's that observant nature that makes me a good detective and what got me promoted to lieutenant at the early age of twenty-nine last year. My attention to detail is a trait of mine that has served me well in this life. I'd like to teach that bitch a lesson or two about paying fucking attention to important details.

I'm about to leave the room when I notice that the nameplate on my desk has been moved. With an annoyed grunt, I adjust the metal so Lieutenant Kasper Grant is perfectly straight. Whichever fucking asshole did this, I'm going to hurt. A smile plays at my lips knowing it was probably Rhodes. I'll get the prick back later.

I shut my office door and lock it before striding down the hallway. As I pass Chief's doorway, he calls out to me.

"Ghost, can you come here a second?"

With a sigh, I turn and stride into his office. His face is contorted into a frown as he stares at his phone. I wait patiently until his features relax, and then he regards me, a brilliant bullshit smile on his face. He thinks he can fool me along with everyone else. But he forgets that I've known him forever. I know his shiny smiles and easygoing personality are anything but genuine. They're forced. All a part of what comes with his prestigious job as police chief. Who the hell am I to judge, though? People change. Apparently Logan wants to be someone nicer now. He's got the whole town fooled, so I guess he's doing a pretty damn good job.

"You headed home?" he asks as he tucks his phone into the breast pocket of his white button-up dress shirt. The pin on his shirt that displays his name, Chief Logan Baldwin, sits neat and straight. It's one of the reasons I get along with Logan. He too sees the value in the details. Together, we've brainstormed on some tricky-ass cases and have found answers many of our detectives had overlooked. I may not believe his plastic smiles, but he's a damn good cop. That I can respect.

"I'm going to head up to The Joint and visit Mom for a bit," I tell him as I run my fingers through my overgrown, almost black hair. I need to get it cut but ever since I fucked Regina over the product bar of the salon after hours a couple of weeks ago, she's been clingy and downright stalking my ass. If I go in to get my hair cut, she'll want to suck my dick or who knows what else. And quite frankly, she wasn't very good at it the first time. I'm not eager for a second go. I'll just have to take my ass to Quick Cuts or have Ashley do it next time I visit.

"Ah, The Joint. Dale going to be there?" he questions, his brows furrowing. We both fucking hate Dale. Due to a conflict of interest, I'm not allowed to personally haul Dale in, being that he's my stepfather and all. But, on the several occasions, when he's whipped up on Mom, and she's called me crying, I've had Logan handle the hauling for me. It's one thing for your boss to know you're the product of a white trash family. It's a whole other thing for all of your subordinates to know, too. Most of these assholes don't like taking orders from "the kid," as some of them call me. If they knew about my fucked-up family, they'd be more than glad to hold that over my head and I'd lose any and all respect that I've worked my ass off to gain. So Logan steps in when I need him to and I owe him big for that.

"Probably. I'll try not to kill him," I joke. "What do you need?"

"Can you ride by Jimmy Salem's building? He's out of town on business. Called and said one of his neighbors told him she'd seen some kids trying to break in. Probably just that, kids, but take a look for me, will you? Jimmy and I go way back, so I told him we'd check it out. I'd do it myself but I have to deal with something rather urgent." He stands and slides on his jacket.

"Sure," I tell him as I turn to leave. "See you tomorrow."

His desk phone rings and soon, he's barking out orders to one of the uniforms. Leaving him to deal with the issue on his own, I stride out of the building toward my department-issued Camaro. Logan and I drive the only two unmarked police cars in the department, whereas the rest of the guys drive typical squad cars. When he'd handed me the keys to the black muscle machine, I nearly fucking died. I'd always heard police departments were lacking on funds.

Not ours.

Somehow, Logan manages to garner substantial

support from the community. With his inherent charm and good looks, he smiles his way into some big-ass donations.

Hell, I'm not complaining.

I hit the button to unlock the vehicle and it beeps in response. As I climb into the car, my thoughts go back to *her*. The one who was too stupid to remember a license plate. Or to recall one tiny fucking detail that could have led the police to my sister. Anyfuckingthing.

Picking up my iPod, I flip through my music until I find "(Don't Fear) The Reaper" by Blue Oyster Cult and then set off on my ride.

I wonder where the hell she's been these last three years. I've stalked her social media accounts and even watched Donovan's office at the lodge, hoping she might show up there one day. Nothing. She's completely gone off the grid. I even briefly considered interrogating Donovan on her whereabouts, but I know he would only lawyer up and refuse to answer like he does with everything else. Then, I'd have Logan on my ass which I don't need. If Logan knew I was still obsessing over this case from nearly a decade ago, he'd probably order a psych evaluation.

I don't need a psych evaluation.

I just need my sister back.

I'm lost in thoughts of her while I make a pass through Jimmy Salem's parking lot. A few beer cans litter the place, evidence of some kids having a recent party, but nothing looks disturbed. After a quick sweep, flashing my light to the dark corners of the building, I pull back on the road to head toward The Joint. My mind is numb once again as I contemplate where she's gone.

As I slow at a four-way stop sign, something big and white comes barreling through off to my right, headlights bouncing as it nears. My eyes zero in on the big-ass Ford 250 which is speeding toward the intersection with no signs of stopping. It plows past me and as it flies past, I recognize the vinyl king's crown decal on the back window that's revealed under the red brake light.

No fucking way.

I pop my flasher on the dash and peel out after the vehicle. Sure enough, as I follow behind it, I recognize the truck to be Logan's. Problem is, I know he's driving the department issue Tahoe today, not his truck.

Did someone actually steal the police chief's vehicle?

What a fucking moron.

Adrenaline surges through my veins as I speed

after the truck. It doesn't show any signs of slow-ing even though I'm tailing its ass with my red and blue lights flashing. I end up following it for a half mile before I realize that whoever's behind the wheel is just driving faster and has no plans to pull over. Knowing there's a curve coming up soon, I yank my wheel to the right and gas it past the truck. As we reach the curve, driving side by side, I start inching into the right lane. I don't want to damage mine or Logan's vehicle but I'm not about to let this person get away. When I barely bump the side of the truck, it jerks off to the right and sails into a ditch. Slamming on my brakes, I pull off to the side a little ways ahead of the truck and jump out of the car. Headlights blind me, so I draw out my 9 mm Glock and aim it at the vehicle.

"Hands on the steering wheel!" I shout as I slow-ly make my way to the truck.

Since it's getting dark, I can't see through the windshield. The hairs stand up on the back of my neck as I approach. Whoever it is, the fucker is going to pay for making me scratch up my car.

When I reach the driver's side window, I peer in. A woman with dark hair is slumped over the steer-ing wheel. My heart thunders in my chest as I tap the glass with my weapon.

"Ma'am," I bark out, "put your hands where I can see them."

Her body quakes and I wonder if she's having a goddamned seizure. With eyes on her, I yank on the door handle. The door swings open and all hell breaks loose. She launches herself at me, knocking my gun from my hand but not before a shot fires off into the trees. As soon as my ass hits the grass, she scrambles to her feet and takes off in a sprint. With a grunt, I jump to my feet, scoop up my gun, and begin running after her.

"Stop or I'll shoot!" I snarl after her as I charge in her direction.

She's short, probably a good six inches shorter than my six-foot frame but she runs like the devil. The headlights shining on her reveal toned legs beneath a floral print dress and cowboy boots. How the fuck she's running in boots is beyond me.

I close in on her, my legs eating up the distance easily, and I tackle her to the dirt.

"Ah!" she cries out the moment her face impacts the ground.

I shove a knee against the small of her back and wrangle her squirming arms into cuffs. As soon as she's secured, I roll her over onto her back so I can Mirandize her. "You have the right to remain—"

She spits in my face, silencing me. "Let me go! I have to go! Now!"

Her panicked tone sends my heart thudding in my chest. But when I push her hair out of her face and lock eyes with her dark, chocolate-colored orbs, my heart ceases to beat. Familiar rage chases away my moment of shock and I fist my hands at my sides.

I fucking found her.

Sweet Nadia Jayne all grown up.

Anger consumes me and I grab her jaw with my fingers, biting into her flesh hard enough to make her yelp.

"You're going to jail you stupid, stupid woman. You stole the police chief's truck," I sneer and bare my teeth at her.

My fingers twitch to grip her neck and choke the fucking life out of her. Fuck serve and protect. More like punish and abuse when it comes to Nadia Jayne.

"Please," she begs, hot tears running from her eyes. "You don't understand. I need to get out of here."

I release her jaw and smirk. "You're not going anywhere except to the station where I'll fingerprint your ass and your rich little daddy can have fun trying to bail you out."

Her eyes widen in horror. "You know Donovan?

Please don't call him. I'm begging you, from one decent human being to another. He can't know I'm here in Aspen. You don't understand..."

A niggling inside of me causes me to take pause. I don't like the way she pleads with me—the way it works its way inside of me. This dumb bitch has the tongue of a goddamned serpent. She let my sister disappear and I cannot forget that.

Ignoring her, I pull my phone out and call Logan. "You'll never believe this," I say with a laugh. "I'm straddling a woman who stole your truck. Donovan Jayne's kid. Can you believe it? I'd like to see him buy his way out of—"

"You have Nadia?" His tone is cool, not at all what I expected.

"I have her detained on Plantation Road, by The Joint. She tried to fucking flee, Logan," I snap, my anger returning like a storm thundering in.

He curses into the phone. "Get her off the ground, goddammit. I'll be there in ten minutes."

When I hang up and shove my phone back into my pocket, I look down to find her face contorted into one of those ugly-cry expressions chicks sometimes make. It irritates me and I want to really give her something to fucking cry about. If I kicked her in the face like that prick who stole my sister did nine years ago, I wonder if she'd forget this whole scene too.

Her supposed forgetful nature seems like such a cop-out.

I would make sure she never forgot the way my boot felt as I crushed her skull.

"Get up," I snap as I rise to my feet dragging her up with me.

She's a fucking mess—her hair a wild entanglement of leaves and snot running from her nose all over her face.

"What did you do?" she questions through her hiccupping sobs.

I frown at her. "I did my job."

She hangs her head in defeat and stays that way until Logan's Tahoe comes barreling down the road toward us. He screeches to a halt and climbs out. Nadia stiffens in my grip but doesn't lift her gaze to meet his. His glare is hateful when his eyes shift to me, and I stare at him, dumbfounded for a moment. I don't get a chance to ask him what the hell is going on because after another second, he shoulders past me and pulls her into his arms.

"Oh, baby," he coos and strokes her hair. "Are you okay?"

She breaks down, as in knees collapsing, gut

wrenching wails kind of breaking down, and it makes me sick. I don't know what's going on but I do know she's playing him. What she did was illegal and I stand behind chasing her ass. The part about wanting to choke her to death was for my own personal vendetta.

"Look, Chief," I mutter to Logan, "she ran a stop sign and was going well over the posted thirty-five miles per hour speed limit. When I finally ran her off the road, she attacked me, ran, and then resisted arrest."

He turns and glares at me as if he wasn't listening to a word I just said. "Un-cuff her."

Clenching my jaw, I yank my key out and unlock the cuffs. Her hands are trembling. This bitch is good. *Too good.* "Now what?"

"She's my Dale," he says, and nods his head over in the direction of The Joint, just down the road. "This is between us, Ghost. Just like it's between us when I have to deal with your stepfather beating the shit out of your mother. *Nadia* stays between us. Do you understand?"

I give him a clipped nod but my gaze falls on her. "You doing a favor for Donovan?"

His Cheshire cat grin doesn't escape me, even though it's quick. He slips his hands into her messy hair and tilts her head back. I watch in shock as he kisses her softly on the lips. Her lip wobbles but she kisses him back, her breathy sigh echoing in the dark. When they finish their weird-ass kiss, he turns to me, a confident smile spread across his face.

"Lieutenant," he says with a chuckle, "meet my fiancée. Cat's officially out of the bag."

And things just got a million times more complicated.

Two

Nadia

Logan Baldwin is a goddamned liar.

And an oh-so-good one, too.

I listened with a mix of awe and horror as he revealed to the man named Ghost that I was his fiancée. On one hand, I should be fist pumping the air. Joyous for such a leap of progress toward my ultimate goal. But I'm not. Instead, I'm terrified of the wrath that will inevitably follow.

We've gone public.

Going public means all eyes on us.

Donovan and Mamá back in my life. A vision of Donovan's pained, steely grey-blue eyes is at the forefront of my mind. Those eyes haunt me but they also remind me—they remind me of my purpose.

He'll come for me eventually.

The thought it is both terrifying and pleasing in one confusing mix of emotions.

It is absolutely crucial, though, that he stays away. I *need* for him to stay away.

"The axel's broken," Logan grunts from his position, crouched on his hands and knees as he peers under his truck.

My heart rate picks up when he stands back up and saunters over to Ghost. The other officer's eyes haven't strayed from mine. I hate the way he stares at me—like he can see into my head, the same head that holds the secrets I'm desperate to protect. Having people find out about Logan and I could be a good thing. But something tells me I'll need to keep my distance from the man with the jade-colored, knowing eyes and unsmiling face.

I shiver, the night air chilling my bones as the adrenaline wears off. Ghost frowns at me. And Logan snaps his head over to me, his eyes flickering with that rage he masks so well.

The sound of Logan clearing his throat breaks the silence that had fallen over us. "Call a tow truck, will you? I need to get Nadia home. She's freezing to death out here. Just have Bill invoice me."

Ghost nods and pulls his cell from his pocket, his gaze never leaving mine. When Logan touches the small of my back to guide me back to the Tahoe, I flinch. His gentle fingers barely brushing against my lower back are more terrifying than his heavy hand.

I remain quiet as he helps me into the vehicle. He climbs in a few seconds later, and soon we're weaving down the dark road. Chewing on my lip, I try to formulate the right words. Words I hope will keep him calm.

The eagle-eyed cop fades in the side mirror as silence fills the Tahoe. The ominous mood surrounding us darkens the night further. "You do realize what you've done, don't you?" he questions in a measured tone, his eyes on the road and both hands gripping the steering wheel tightly.

My heart rate quickens and I let out a small whimper. "Logan, please... I swear on everything I love that I'll play the part for you. They'll never know."

His eyes dart over to mine for a moment before they're back on the road again. "Oh, believe me, I have no doubt about that. You're going to have to convince everyone in this whole goddamned town about your depth of feeling for me. No backing down now."

My hands tremble in my lap. I quickly clasp them together so he doesn't pick up on the overwhelming fear that nearly consumes me. Logan feeds off of fear and I don't want to strengthen the beast. I need to weaken him. Use the skills I've perfected over time and make him feel reassured.

"I promise I'll be perfect for you, Logan."

He nods and the rest of the drive is silent. I know in that twisted head of his, he's contemplating my punishment. Beatings. Whippings. Orgasm deprivation. Near suffocation over and over again.

Those are preferable.

Always my choice.

Because when it comes to Logan, he knows my weaknesses. With Logan, his psychological punishments are much worse. He knows my Achilles heel and isn't afraid to cut me where it hurts the most.

"Donovan is going to be a problem," he says as he puts on the blinker to turn into his driveway. "I'm going to have to figure out how to deal with that one." The moonlight shines down on the large, stunning estate. If it wasn't the place that housed my worst nightmares, I'd be in love with the architectural beauty of it. It's a delicate mix of rustic country meets modern elegance, which is a common décor choice here in Aspen among the wealthy.

And Logan is among the wealthy. He's practically their leader amid the local Aspen community. Well, he and Donovan are.

He tells everyone he's a trust fund kid—because clearly, he couldn't ever afford a house like this on a police chief's salary. And just like all of his other lies, they believe it. There was a time when I trusted and believed in him too.

Until he turned my world upside down.

He pulls into his three-car garage beside "The Beast," as he calls that vehicle. The space where his truck once sat remains empty. As soon as the overhead door closes, caging us inside of his fortress, I swallow down the panic flopping around in my belly like a fish on the bank. It's time to breathe and face the music. And this isn't the good kind of music. No Led Zeppelin here crooning away in my head. Instead, raging Pantera is what threatens to crush me.

But the time for crying is over.

The armor is going up.

This warrior princess is strapping up for battle.

"How will you punish me?" I question when I climb out of the Tahoe and slam the door.

He's already striding into the house, ignoring my words. I trot after him, hoping to distract him in some way from the inevitable. By the time I make it into his room, he's yanking off his tie and tossing it on the bed. With practiced finesse, he pops each button on his white dress shirt until it's completely undone and he peels it from his muscled frame.

Logan is forty-five years old, the same age as Donovan, and has the body of a thirty-year-old. He's lean in all the right places but his muscles are more sculpted and defined on his arms, shoulders, and abs. As he stands in his slacks and white sleeveless undershirt, I admire his monstrous beauty. Despite the undershirt covering up most of his body, his sleeve of tattoos on his left arm is visible and my eyes fixate on the words.

Harmony after annihilation.

Those words are my focus. When he does his worst, I focus on those words. My constant reminder.

Just like now.

His tattoos are a colorful piece of artwork surrounding that profound phrase. The phoenix which takes up most of his arm bears his dark eyes, symbolic of the man before me. Within the flames permanently licking his skin encompassing the hellish bird are names. Reminders. My reasons. I fixate on my favorite one and steel my heart, preparing myself for annihilation.

"Logan, what are you going to do? You're too quiet."

He peels off the undershirt and once again, my eyes are drawn to his masculine physique. More tattoos cover his chest and abdomen. His chest is mostly free of hair aside from the dark trail centered in the V of his lower abdomen.

The man is beautiful.

But on the inside, he's a wolf in sheep's clothing.

Wicked darkness cloaked in smiling light.

And yet, I still have a sick, sliver of love for him.

It doesn't make sense, but when his dark, familiar eyes meet mine, it does. I can look past those menacing eyes and see perfection. Beauty. Innocence. It's pure—untainted and uncorrupted—and I'd do anything for that untarnished part of him.

"Who says I want to punish you?" he questions, the thick cord of muscle on his neck tightening.

Dread washes over me and I rush over to him. "Please, Logan. I'm begging you. Hurt me."

His gaze meets mine and he smirks. I hate his smirks. When I hear the jingle of his belt, I nearly sob in relief. But when he yanks it from the loops of his pants and wraps it tightly around his fist, panic once again chokes me. He pushes past me, out of his bedroom and down the hallway. I know where he's going. I can't let things escalate that far.

"No!" I cry out and launch myself against his back before he reaches the door to the basement. "Not down there. For the love of God, just fuck me up. Fuck me up on the kitchen floor or your bed or the back porch. I don't care. Just do it up here."

He shakes me off of him and I slip between him and the door. His eyes are darkened with rage and his breathing is so heavy he's visibly shaking. Desperate to distract him from what I know is coming, I grab his thick cock through his work slacks.

"Choke me with your cock, Logan," I beg with fat tears welling in my eyes.

He laughs, the sound cruel and humorless. "I'm not in a choking mood."

I grab on to his fist holding the belt and stand on my toes to try and meet his vacant glare. "Make me bleed," I implore him firmly, rapidly blinking the tears away. "Make me bleed with this." I squeeze the leather he's holding and then lick my lips.

His anger lessens marginally and his features slightly relax. I pounce, not wasting any time, and wrap my arms around his neck. He dips his head to meet my lips and I kiss him hard. I throw all of my energy into distracting him from breaking my soul a little more than he already has.

I'm a wolf too, you see.

The games Logan plays are no longer difficult to understand.

In fact, sometimes I think I'm starting to win.

His tongue spears into my mouth and I let out a moan as he kisses me hungrily. And I am pleased for the simple fact he's reciprocating. When I hop to wrap my short legs around his firm waist, he grabs on to my ass with a punishing grip. I yelp, which only spurs him on because he loves to hear me scream and he strides away from the basement toward his bedroom. My heart leaps into my throat because his bedroom is the safest room in the house. It means he's feeling softer than usual which surprises me.

Maybe I'm finally getting to him.

When we finally reach his bed, he pushes me onto it. I bounce on the mattress and then jerk my gaze to his, waiting for his next move. He starts undressing the rest of the way, baring his large cock to me, but I wait patiently for his next order.

"Leave the boots on. Everything else goes," he says, his tone curt, as he takes his cock in his free hand.

I focus on the way he strokes himself as I go up on my knees to peel off my dress. At one time, his dick had been too big. Too scary. Too much. It'd been enough punishment alone. But over time, I grew used to the way he filled and stretched every hole in my body. I'd learned how to turn myself on so I could accept him more easily. It was the only way. With Logan, you just have to accept that he's going to destroy you from the inside out. Once I finally made peace with that, it soon became easier to take all of the crooked, brutal parts of him.

"Now, lie face down across the bottom of the bed."

I scramble to heed his instructions and wait for the pain that will inevitably come. But then it doesn't come. Not right away. Instead, he teases my flesh by dragging the leather of his belt along my spine toward my ass. I focus on the way it tickles my skin and imagine his mouth on my clit, sucking and tasting. Just the idea of him between my legs has me growing wet.

I absolutely need to be wet.

"Did you get the shit you needed from the store?" he asks softly.

I shudder at his tone but nod. "Yeah, it's in my purse. I can add it to the meal and then put it in the oven as soon as you're done with my punishment."

Crack!

Fire rips across my skin as the belt cracks against

my ass. I scream but don't dare move. His heavy hand is more preferable than the other implements he has at his disposal.

"One thing, doll. You had to get one thing. What took you so long? Do I need to remind you what happens when you run late?" he demands with a hiss, his finger flicking the sore flesh where he whipped me.

Gritting my teeth against the pain, I shake my head emphatically. "I never need a reminder. You know that. It was the stupid train. I was doing great on time until the train held me up. Please," I beg, "you have to believe me."

"*Hmmmm...* If you aren't guilty, then why are you begging for punishment?" His question throws me off guard and I stutter trying to find the right answer.

"I, uh, I—"

Crack!

This time his hit lands on the middle of my back and it hurts like hell. I clutch onto the bedding to keep from scrambling away from him. Seeking escape is not an option.

"Tell me why the fuck I'm whipping you, Nadia, if you're so fucking innocent," he seethes, his breath coming out in ragged huffs.

A sob gets caught in my throat but I swallow it down. "B-B-Because I like it when you hurt me," I lie and push my ass into the air. "I need the pain."

Clearly, I'm a masochist. But I have my reasons.

"Is that so?" he questions with a chuckle and runs the leather of his belt down along the crack of my ass. "Are you wet?"

"Yes," I tell him, "and I crave for you to fuck me."

He pops my ass playfully with the belt and I squeak in surprise. I was expecting another lashing. But then his fingers, two of his thick digits, are pushing into my pussy, completely distracting me from any thoughts of punishment. He glides them in and out easily because my being wet for him wasn't a lie. My body is under my command and I can control it as needed.

"Lie down on your back in the middle of the bed," he says suddenly as he wrenches his fingers from inside me.

Without hesitation, I scramble over to the middle of the bed and wince when I lay down on my newly inflicted welts. His dark eyes peruse over my large breasts, down over my flat tummy and wide hips, to my pussy.

"So beautiful. How'd you manage to trick me into becoming my fiancée?" he questions as he climbs on to the bed. He gently spreads my knees apart and hooks my legs around his waist. I swallow down my anxiety when he loops the belt around my neck. It isn't tight...*yet*.

"I didn't trick you. I just want to be with you all the time. I'm glad people will know I belong to you," I tell him with a practiced smile.

He yanks on the belt hard enough to pull me into a sitting position by my neck. My fingers naturally claw at the leather to loosen its grip. The air I was so easily breathing seconds before is completely cut off and my tongue hangs out as if in a search of just one tiny breath.

"Damn straight you belong to me," he snarls as he uses his other hand to guide me onto his cock. I slide down easily over him and he grunts in pleasure. "It'll be a nightmare, though, once Donovan gets wind of this. He doesn't share well."

Stars are glittering in my vision as I struggle to breathe. My first reaction is to get rid of the belt, but when I can't loosen it, I grab on to the back of his hair and attempt to pull him from me. He hisses at me but doesn't release me. Instead, he slams us down on the bed and he fucks me into the mattress, his grip never waning on the belt. When I go to push at his face to get him to release my throat, he bares his teeth to my forearm and bites down like a wild beast.

More searing pain jolts through me but I can't

scream. My sobs, my screams, my pleas are all lodged in my throat below where the belt is cutting them off. I can feel the blood trickling down my arm and I start to grow dizzy.

My body goes limp beneath him. I don't remember him coming. I fade off into the darkness of my mind. It's warm and quiet there. Safe. *He's* there.

"That's not a word." His eyebrow is arched up in challenge.

I stare at the Scrabble board and frown. "Where I come from, it is."

He smirks and shakes his head. "The things I allow…"

Smiling triumphantly, I accept all sixty-four points. "Your turn, loser."

His eyes are on the board and I take a moment to risk a glance at him. I like when he's relaxed and playful. "Keep talking, little girl. I'll still win and then what?"

"You're not going to win," I scoff.

His lips quirk up into a smile and he tugs at the knot in his tie, loosening it. The action steals my attention for a moment. "And if I do?"

Heat burns up my neck as a brief, wicked thought flits through my head. One I'd never allow myself to say aloud. I swallow down my embarrassment and meet his stare.

"You won't. But I'll humor you. If you do, what do you want?"

He reaches across the table to pull some tiles from the bag and accidentally brushes his hand against mine. Just an accident. I think. *My cheeks must be blazing crimson at this point but a jolt of excitement courses through me at his touch. Our eyes meet, his searching mine with an unexpected heat behind them. Such an intense, foreign heat.* I think. "If I win, you have to..." *He looks off, somewhere behind me, as if he were considering this seriously.* "Wash my car."

I'm already shaking my head and arguing. "It's ninety degrees out there, easily!"

He contemplates my words and his lips twitch with amusement. "You can wear your swimsuit if you want. I'm easy. You know I'd never let you suffer." *At this, he winks. Playfully.* I think.

I clench my thighs together and refrain from fanning the heat away from me, which seems to have crept inside on this unusually warm late October evening. "I'm going to win," *I assure him.* I think.

But then, I spend his entire next move wondering how I can let him catch up. Because, I do, in fact want to lose. Anything to see that hungry look in his eyes when he mentioned me wearing my bathing suit. And he was hungry. For me. I think.

I think *I want him to see me like that, barely dressed. And I'm not sure why.*

I think *he wants to see me like that, barely dressed. And I'm not sure why.*

"Mine," *he says in a low, gravelly voice, which makes me shiver.*

My eyes fly to his in shock but then I stupidly realize "mine" was his word, not a declaration... of any other sort. Oh. However, there's no mistaking the glint in his eyes. Primal and shameless. Starved. For me. I think.

He most definitely wants me.

I think.

Does it make me a bad person if I think *I want him too?*

"Shhh," his deep voice coos as I drag my eyelids open, stealing me from my warm memories.

He's still inside of me but he's removed the belt from my neck. His eyes shine with something I've never seen before. Adoration maybe? Pride?

My throat is hoarse and scratchy. I'd kill for some water right now but I'm too weak to move. I tense when he starts peppering kisses all over my face and then down along my sore throat. He makes his way to my collarbone and when he reaches the top of my full breast, he sucks the upper part of it hard into his mouth. I want to cry out but I'm too worn out to do much protesting. He sucks and sucks until I know I'll have a big-ass bruise for days.

"I'm ready for dinner, doll. I have some cases to look over but I want to watch you cook in nothing but those cowboy boots you're wearing," he says with a playful growl. "So fucking hot."

He climbs off of me and saunters off toward the bathroom, his sculpted ass tightening with each step. I attempt to sit up and manage to bring my shaky hand toward me to examine it properly. His teeth marks left a red, angry mark, and in some parts of his bite, he punctured the skin. Blood continues to seep from the wounds and I can only stare at it.

I don't realize he's returned until he pulls my hand from my gaze. His brows furrow as he inspects the wound. My belly flops when he brings my wrist to his mouth. I brace myself for him to hurt me again but instead, he runs his tongue along the flesh and licks up the blood. He flashes me a wolfish smile.

"Clean this up so it doesn't get infected," he instructs and climbs off the bed to start dressing. "Wrap it in some gauze and then start dinner. I'm fucking starving."

I let out a relieved sigh the moment he leaves the

bedroom and dutifully do as he says. It isn't until I've cleaned my arm and am wrapping it in gauze that I allow myself to smile in celebration of my small victory.

I did it.

I fucking did it.

Logan was enraged beyond logical reason, yet I had the ability to bring him back down to earth. To me. This is progress. We may be going public with our relationship, but I won't let that ruin my carefully laid out plans. It'll be trickier, especially when Donovan assuredly shows up, but I have do this.

I need to do this.

My heart depends on it.

The fragility of my perfectly sculpted plan is hanging precariously in the balance of others who could ruin everything. People are nosy, especially the good-looking cop who ran me off the road. His eyes were calculating. Perceptive. Aware. Not one who seems to miss a single detail. I just pray to God I can fool him too.

The lives of the ones I love depend on my ability to play a part.

Sweet Jayne is available now!

Made in the USA
Columbia, SC
18 October 2017